Death From Unnatural Causes

An Al Pennyback Mystery

by

Charles Ray

huru pres

For information about this and other works of this author, contact the author at charlesray.author@yahoo.com. .

Printed in the United States of America,

ISBN: 0615766234
ISBN-13: 978-01615766232 (Uhuru Press)

Other books by this author

Al Pennyback Mysteries
Color Me Dead
Memorial to the Dead
Deadline
Dead, White, and Blue
The Day the Music Died
If I Should Die Before I Wake
A Good Day to Die
Die, Sinner
Death by Design
Deadly Intentions
Till Death Do Us Part
Deadly Dose
Dead Man's Cove
Dead Men Don't Answer

Other Fiction
Angel on His Shoulder
She's No Angel
Child of the Flame
Pip's Revenge
Wallace in Underland
Further Adventures of Wallace in Underland
Buffalo Soldier: Trial by Fire
Buffalo Soldier: Homecoming
Buffalo Soldier: Incident at Cactus Junction
Buffalo Soldier: Peacekeepers
Dead Letter and Other Tales

Non-fiction
Things I Learned from My Grandmother About Leadership and Life

Taking Charge: Effective Leadership for the Twenty-first Century

African Places: A Photographic Journey Through Zimbabwe and Southern Africa

Grab the Brass Ring

Charles Ray

DEDICATION

To all the dedicated, professional care
givers for the elderly and infirm, who labor
often anonymously. My hat's off to you.

ACKNOWLEDGMENTS

The idea for this book came from many sources.
First and foremost, conversations with my son,
David and my daughter, Denise quite often give me
inspiration for stories; thanks guys. But, I have to
say, the main inspiration for the current tale has to
go to my granddaughter, Samantha, who is the light
of my life, but who has brought home in the
starkest terms that, despite my best efforts, I'm
getting old.

Chapter 1

I have always had a problem dealing with kids and old people. Since the death of my son, Ethan, killed when he was six, along with his mother and several of his soccer teammates when a truck driver ran a stop sign and T-boned the van my wife Sarah was driving, bringing them back from an evening soccer game in Northern Virginia, I've avoided children as much as possible. I'm godfather to my friend Buster Mayweather's twins, a boy and a girl, but I don't have to be around them all that much, so it hasn't presented much of a problem. As for the elderly, one would think that as I approach my own fiftieth birthday, it wouldn't be an issue. One would be wrong. Other than my grandmother, who never acted her age until she died at the age of ninety-six, and Carlton Raine, an octogenarian who is retired from the CIA, I haven't had to be around old people much. Raine, whose nickname is 'Blood,' for some pretty gory reasons, has been living with a woman 47 years his junior for over a year, so it's hard to think of him as old. If you saw Elizabeth Sung, a lawyer I'd introduced him to, you'd think he was the young one; she always has a satisfied look on her face.

I'm a private investigator, 49 years old, and I've been running my own agency, with the help of my trusty assistant, Heather Bunche, for a little over a decade. We're on retainer to the law firm of Holcombe, Stein and Chang, in which my old army buddy, Quincy Chang, is the junior partner. Mostly I track down missing heirs, deadbeat clients, and do the occasional background check for them; not really demanding or dangerous work, but, along with the fees we get from the occasional case that comes over the transom, it pays the rent, utilities, Heather's salary, and leaves a little over for me. I don't spend much; taking care of my living expenses with my army retirement pay.

It's not that I don't respect age, you understand; I just don't know how to deal with it.

So, I found myself wondering what the hell I was doing at the Shady Grove Retirement Center in Rockville, Maryland, surrounded by a group of people that were old when I was born, considering one of the over-the-transom cases.

Tucked away behind a large stand of oak trees on a gently sloping hillside west of I-270 and just south of Maryland Route 28, Shady Grove Retirement Center looked like any other suburban neighborhood when you first drove past the stone cairns that sat to either side of the entrance. A sprawling compound, the large administration building sat in the center; a one-story white stone building with gray slate roof, it was encircled by stands of oak, chestnut, pine, and cedar trees crowned with lush green foliage that in mid-May was in full bloom. Low, neatly trimmed azaleas, emblazoned with red blossoms, framed the base of the L-shaped building. Several smaller structures, wood frame one-story box shapes, painted in various pastel colors and with green, brown, and rust-red slate roofs, were situated around the central building, and connected to it by winding stone walkways. Crows, cardinals, and blue jays flitted through the trees and hopped about the grounds, competing with the squirrels for grubs and other insects in the immaculately manicured grass. It was, at first glance, an idyllic setting. Once you were inside the compound, though, it hit you like a kidney punch; everyone was old, pale, frail, and bent, except for the young, sun-bronzed complexioned and, hearty-looking attendants in their powder blue uniforms, who floated around and among the residents.

There seemed to be about one attendant for each ten elderly residents; and, from what I'd been told, there were just a hundred residents. Shady Grove was an exclusive retirement community; something called an assisted living community; but, if you were dependent solely upon your social security check, you need not apply for residence. It was for those who had independent means, but who were no longer able to care for themselves, and who didn't have family capable or willing to take care of them.

I pulled my Mustang into an empty space in the small parking lot at the left front of the large building which was marked for staff and visitors. There were four other cars, a black Mercedes, a silver BMW, and two silver Toyota SUVs, parked in slots marked for staff. There were no visitors' cars.

I pushed through the double glass doors, entering a large reception area with plush couches and plastic chairs scattered around. Low tables that looked like mahogany, but upon closer inspection were actually plastic with faux wood patterns, with magazines and newspapers idly scattered on their surfaces, were placed in close proximity to the chairs and couches. A few hunched seniors, some staring at the walls, while others thumbed idly through the publications, were sitting in the area. Except for the occasional crackle of a newspaper page being turned, and the scuffing sound of the crepe soles of the shoes worn by the attendants, the place was as silent as a mausoleum.

A young, sun-tanned blonde; her hair pulled back into a pony tail, sat behind a kidney-shaped desk with a glass top. She was thumbing through a fashion magazine, looking as bored as everyone else in the room. She looked up at me as I approached the desk, and folded the page she'd been reading.

"May I help you?" she asked. She looked to be in her early twenties, but had the voice of a pre-teen, reedy and nasal. Her eyes were bright blue behind fluffy bronze lashes.

I showed her my ID. The photo on it is ten years old, so the gray at my temples is not evident; but, it still looks like me.

"I'm Al Pennyback," I said. "I'm here to see William Powderly."

"Mr. Powderly is probably somewhere on the grounds with his friends. If you'll have a seat, I'll have someone find him."

She waved at one of the orderlies, a young black man with weightlifter's shoulders. When he came over, she asked him to find Powderly and inform him he had a visitor.

I sat in one of the plastic chairs near the reception desk. The newspaper on the nearby table was a week-old *Washington Post*, and next to it was a wrinkled copy of *National Geographic*, neither of which interested me, so I sat back and subtly scanned the room. The receptionist had her head buried in her magazine, moving her lips as she read whatever article she was reading. About two chairs away, an old woman with rounded shoulders draped in a pink shawl, her stringy white hair hanging over her brow, sat staring at the floor. Her withered lips were moving, but no sound came out of her mouth, just a little dribble of spit that hung out of the corner.

After about five minutes, the black orderly came back, followed by a tall man with long muscular arms and a burnished complexion like polished wood, dressed in khaki pants, a red and black plaid shirt and wearing work boots. His dark brown face was heavily lined, and there were large bags under his dark brown eyes. His crinkly white hair was cropped close to his square head.

"You're that Al Pennyback fella my niece said was comin' to see me?" he asked. His voice was deep and resonant.

I stood and offered my hand. His grip was strong and dry.

"Yes," I said. "Your niece is a friend of my assistant. She said you had a problem that you needed my help with."

"That I do. Corinne; that's my niece; said you were the man to talk to if you had a problem you couldn't solve."

That, unfortunately, is my problem; over the years, my penchant for taking on cases that have befuddled the police, and having the results of my investigations chronicled by Lucy Mendez, a feature writer for the *Washington Post*, has led to the general belief that I can do it when others fail. It's led to me being plopped into the middle of all kinds of strangeness.

"It depends on the problem," I said. "What happens to be yours?"

His face furrowed and he glanced around the room. "Not here. Let's go outside and I'll tell you all about it."

He turned and headed for the door, not bothering to see if I was following. He had the manners of someone who was accustomed to having people follow his orders. After driving all the way from my office in Southwest DC, not far from Washington Channel, I figured I might as well humor him. I got up and followed. The young orderly who'd fetched him for me shrugged and gave me a look that mirrored how I was feeling.

The old man walked along a stone path that wound between the azalea bushes, ending in a circular area fenced by pines and chestnuts. Two stone benches sat on the rim of a little fish pond in which two orange looking carp swam around in lazy circles. Two people, a slightly pudgy white man with a thick thatch of white hair that needed trimming, and a tiny woman with a hawk nose and dark blue eyes, sat on one of the benches.

"Is this him?" the woman asked as we entered the little bower. "He the one that's gonna help us?"

"Don't know," my escort said. "Haven't told him what we want him to do yet."

He ushered me to the empty bench, taking a seat on the opposite end. We sat facing the other two.

"Looks a bit too young to be as smart as your niece said," the other man said in a high-pitched, cracking voice.

"I'm almost fifty," I said. I don't know why I said it. My age shouldn't matter; but, for some reason I felt compelled to let it be known that I was no spring chicken myself.

"Hah," he said. "You're still a stripling compared to us. Hell, I was a grown man before you were even a twinkle in your daddy's eye."

"Don't be so hard on the child, George," the woman said.

William Powdery, in a voice that emphasized that he was in charge, said, "Why don't we all just pipe down and let me tell him what we need before we go gradin' him on his ability."

"That would be useful," I said. That earned me a glare from all three.

"Before we get to that," he said. "It'd be helpful if you knew a bit about us, so you won't be thinkin' we're just a bunch of old codgers who are imagining things."

The one thing I've learned after more than a decade as a private eye is that the best way to get information out of people is to let it come out naturally. You can't force it or coerce it, at least not in any useful form. The other thing I've learned is that when people start a conversation with conditions, like thinking you might suspect they're not totally accurate you have to take everything with a shaker of salt, because they're probably *not* being totally accurate.

William Powderly, though, didn't impress me as someone given to flights of fancy. He was 88; a retired mailman who had also invested his money wisely, so he could afford Shady Grove in his declining years. His only relative was his niece, Corinne, a secretary at the Department of Commerce, who had three kids of her own and couldn't take him in. I wasn't too sure about his friends, though. George Tecumseh Madison, 87, looked ten years older than William, and had a habit of darting his eyes around when he spoke as if he thought someone was spying on him. The youngster of the trio, at 82, was Helen Anthony; she'd been a successful commercial artist.

Powderly delivered the information dryly and in a matter-of-fact tone, as if he was inserting letters in suburban mailboxes; something he'd done for more than thirty years.

"We all began living here around the same time," he said. "And, we became friends."

"We all hang out together," Anthony said. "Because, everyone else here's so old and decrepit. All they want to do is sit around reading or talking about old times - -"

"Or grossing you out with detailed descriptions of their bowel movements," Madison said.

They all made faces. I could sympathize with that, but, I also wanted someone to get to the point.

"There were four of us in the group for a long while," Powderly said. "Geraldine; Geraldine Wallace, was sort of the leader because she was the oldest."

"Of course, the way that gal cut a rug," Anthony said. "You'd never know she was ninety. She could run rings around the rest of us."

"She'd been here for a while before the rest of us," Powderly continued. "She sort of took us under her wings after we arrived. I think she was happy to have us here, too, because everybody else is so dull. We all hung out at one or the other's place; we each have one of the cottages, instead of the apartments in the main building; and played cards, listened to music, danced and stuff. Staff used to call us the Four Mouseketeers."

I had a hard time imagining any of them in that role. I must have raised an eyebrow, which I sometimes do when I'm perplexed.

"It's not as silly as you might think," Anthony said. "Just because we're a bit more mature than the average person, it doesn't mean we're incapable of enjoying life."

The men nodded and harrumphed in agreement. I felt appropriately chastised. "Sorry, it's not that I don't believe that each of you can be the life of the party; but, what does this have to do with your need for a private detective?"

"Well," Powderly said. "For a private detective who is supposed to be so good, you don't seem to be all that observant."

"Is there something here I should be seeing?"

"It's not what's here; it's what you don't see, young man," Anthony said. "Bill just told you that we were a close-knit group of four people; yet, you have before you only three. Does that not tell you something?"

"It tells me that your friend, Ms. Wallace was

it, is not here with you. Is there some significance to her absence?"

Sad looks crossed their faces.

"She's not here," Powderly said. "Because she recently passed away."

"My condolences; but, I still don't see how that involves a private investigator. Do you want me to try and locate her heirs or something like that?"

"No, Mr. Pennyback," he said. "We want you to find out who killed her."

Chapter 2

The next hour was spent in a futile effort on my part trying to convince three very determined senior citizens that there was nothing unusual about a ninety-year-old woman dying.

When I asked how she died, Powderly replied that the doctor in charge of medical care at Shady Grove, Morgan Winthrop, who was the resident physician, had said it was from a heart attack. So, I said, she died of natural causes.

"Wasn't nothin' natural about it," he said. "She died of unnatural causes, 'cause somebody killed her."

"You think maybe the doctor did it?"

"Could be; could be any of them."

"Come on," I said. "What would the motive

be? I mean, a suspicious death would turn up something during an autopsy."

"Yeah, if there'd been an autopsy. Thing is, when a physician is present and nothing looks funny, they don't do an autopsy."

That bit of news brought me up short.

"You mean the doctor just declared her dead, and that was that?"

"Yup," Madison said. "And, he signed the death certificate and everything. Just like that, poor Geraldine's dead and done and no one is doing a thing about it."

"Well, couldn't you request the body be exhumed and an autopsy conducted?"

"Sure we could, son," Powderly said. "If there was a body to ex-hume. The home had her cremated. Can't tell too much from ashes."

"That's a bit strange. Did you tell this to the police?"

"Huh! I called the county police. They sent a guy out here to talk to me, but after he spoke to Dr. Winthrop, he treated me like I was some kind of invalid. Said there was no evidence of foul play, and that everything was in order and left. He didn't even take any notes of what I told him."

"Do you know what the doctor told him?"

"Yeah; they said her heart just give out. That she was ninety and had a weak ticker. Horse pocky! That woman was strong as a horse; she had five or six good years left in her; ain't no way she had no stroke."

"When was she cremated?"

"The day after she died. They took her over to the crematorium less than a day after."

"Seems to me that would have raised some suspicion."

"Uh, well, thing is, she signed a paper when she first come here saying she wanted to be cremated. We all have to sign that paper when we come here. That policeman said everything was done according to her wishes, and he didn't see anything that was out of order."

I was still to be convinced that there was a reason for me to be involved, but, one part of my mind was leaning toward it. I have this thing about the way bureaucracies treat people. The tendency of bureaucrats to look for the easy answer and give the little guy the stiff arm to avoid having to do an honest day's work. William Powderly struck me as a straight up kind of guy; someone not given to flights of fancy; and, he seemed sincere in what he was saying and absolutely convinced he was right.

"Let me get this straight," I said. "You check in here, you have to sign a paper giving Shady

Grove the right to dispose of your body when you die?"

"It's not as bad as it sounds." He chuckled. "Most of us don't have any family on the outside, so it makes sense to have the center take care of things when we're gone. Most of us leave everything to the center anyway."

"Whoa; you mean they get your estate? Most of you guys aren't exactly poor, right?"

Helen Anthony laughed; she had a musical voice and her eyes twinkled and her nose wrinkled when she laughed. I found myself liking her. "It might as well go to them as to the government," she said. "Most of us have no family left; unlike Bill here." She nodded toward Powderly. "He'll leave everything to his niece and her family. The rest of us, though, have no one, so it makes sense to help Shady Grove continue to be able to maintain the level of excellent care it offers."

"Yeah," Madison said. "They do everything here. For those of us who can't, or don't want to cook, they prepare meals; they keep our places clean; we even have our own clinic here that can do almost anything short of organ transplant."

"Sounds pretty self-contained," I said.

"It has to be, unfortunately." There was a note of sadness in Powderly's voice. "You'll know what I mean someday, young fella. When you get old in this country, you become a nuisance to everyone around you. Here at Shady Grove, everything's taken care of. We don't have to deal with the rejection of the young world outside."

I wanted to tell him that he was mistaken; but, I knew he wasn't. I recalled my own reaction to being behind an elderly person in the checkout line of a store, as he or she fumbled for change, or forgot something, and only meditation keeps my blood pressure from rising when I have to drive behind a senior driver who insists on going ten miles per hour *below* the limit. We do put a premium on youth; millions spent on forever looking young, as if we can somehow chemically fend off the march of time, fooling ourselves until we wake up one day and find ourselves on the other side of the age line. The thoughts didn't make me feel good about myself.

Maybe it was the guilt at the way I felt about being around old people; the need to atone for my prejudice; or, the fact that I can't resist the opportunity to force the system to pay attention; but, I found myself drifting ever closer to saying I'd take the case.

Not that I thought I could prove anything. I'm no medical expert, and what I know about forensic science wouldn't intimidate first grader; but, I'm pretty good at sussing out the truth, and my mind works in strange ways. It was an interesting puzzle, too; and, I'm a sucker for puzzles. The more impossible, the better.

"Okay, let's say I buy what you're saying; that your friend was murdered; if I take the case, it won't be cheap."

"Son, you weren't listening," Powderly said. "We're not exactly tapped out, and we might as well give it to you as to wait around for this place to get it."

They didn't even blink when I told them my daily fee was two hundred plus expenses. I agreed to take the case; hoping I wouldn't regret it; and told them I'd have my assistant, Heather Bunche, type up a contract and bring it for their signature.

In the meantime, I figured I might as well get a head start on the investigation.

Chapter 3

Morgan Winthrop wasn't exactly the image of a country doctor. He looked, in fact, like someone central casting would send over to play the mad scientist in a budget horror flick.

He was completely bald, his head bulging slightly at the top, with dark, arched brows over cold looking brown eyes that sat to either side of a sharp, straight nose over thin lips. He had one of those beard-mustache combinations; was clean on the cheeks with the 'stache melding into a pointed beard, and a little triangular tuft of hair beneath his lower lip. He was wearing a white hospital gown over dusty blue scrubs. An expensive silver pen was clipped in the breast pocket of the gown.

He sat behind a large teak desk, all curves and carving, with an old fashioned phone sitting next to a laptop computer. Next to the computer was a silver pen holder with two more expensive looking silver pens. His chair was a dark brown, high backed oriental style; probably teak like the desk; with arm rests that ended in dragons' heads and red velvet padding. A couple of lacquer panels hung on the wall to either side of the window behind him, shiny black wood with dragons, flowers and Chinese characters. The rug was red and gold, with black trim, with more dragons and Chinese characters. In front of the desk was another chair, a smaller version of the one in which he sat. At the four corners of the room stood large black lacquer vases, almost my height; again, the dragon and character motif. This guy had a thing for Chinese dragons.

I'd decided to begin my enquiries with the dude who'd been on the scene when Geraldine Wallace died; the doctor who'd pronounced cause of death and signed the death certificate. He didn't appear too happy at being chosen.

"Would you mind telling me how the death of one of our residents would be of interest to a private investigator?" he asked, glaring icily at me over his steepled fingertips. His nails were immaculately manicured. His eyes were like little dots of lacquered teak.

"I've been retained by friends of hers to inquire into the circumstances of her death."

I can be just as hoity toity as the next guy,

and, I had a feeling this was the way he talked. Well, more than a feeling; he *did* talk that way.

"The circumstances were really quite simple. She suffered a, well, to use laymen's terms, a heart attack, followed by a massive stroke."

"Her friends tell me she was in excellent health."

"Her friends; and, I assume you mean Mr. Powderly and his two followers; are not doctors. The woman was ninety years old. She drank, smoked, and had the most horrid diet; we could never get her to eat the food we prepare in the kitchen here; always insisting on preparing her own meals. She was a heart attack waiting to happen."

"Had she been ill before?"

"I'm not in the habit of discussing my patients, or any of the other residents of Shady Grove with strangers, Mr. Pennyback."

"Seeing as how she's dead, doctor-patient privilege hardly applies, don't you think?"

His nose wrinkled as if I'd just broken wind.

"Be that as it may, I don't see why this is your concern."

"When I'm hired to do a job, I do it. I've been hired to determine the true circumstances of Ms. Wallace's death, and, since you're the one who signed the death certificate, I start with talking to you."

"You don't believe that incredible story they're telling, do you? That she didn't die of a heart attack?"

"Doesn't matter what I believe. They believe it, and my job's to look into it. Now; are you sure there couldn't have been some other cause of death?"

"Are you questioning my competence? I'll have you now I've been a physician for twenty years; and attending physician here at Shady Grove for fifteen. I don't make mistakes."

"Come on, doc, everyone makes the occasional mistake."

The icy glare got colder by several degrees.

"I think this interview is over," he said. His voice dripped ice. "I will not have my credentials questioned by someone who has no medical knowledge."

I hadn't been impressed by Winthrop upon entering his office, and his officious manner was lowering my opinion of him by the second. "Look, you can answer my questions and clear the air, or you can put up with me nosing around, making a nuisance of myself; and, in the process maybe drawing unwanted attention to your operation here. It's your call."

I also know when to drop the hoity toity persona and go back to being the hard ass gumshoe who can get in your face and make life miserable. He was clearly not accustomed to being spoken to in that way. His ivory complexion darkened.

"I will not be threatened. If you persist in bothering me I'll contact our lawyer and have a restraining order placed against you."

"You do that, doc; but, while you're waiting for some judge to review the application and issue the order I can make things very uncomfortable for you. It'd be a lot easier if you'd just humor me." I decided to throw him a bone; no sense in totally alienating him this early in the investigation. "If it makes you feel any better, I think you're probably right. But, these people feel marginalized and ignored, and if we can give them answers that they're willing to accept, this goes away, and you're left with a bunch of happy campers."

He tapped a well-manicured forefinger on the desk. Then, he sighed. "Okay; if I agree to cooperate with your, er, inquiry, you'll be discrete? We don't need bad publicity for the center."

"Yeah, I imagine it's bad for business. Sure, I'm the soul of discretion."

"If the news media were to get wind of these baseless allegations, there would be no end to the horrible stories they'd run. They're always trying to say that centers like ours exploit the elderly, and nothing is farther from the truth. We were lucky that didn't happen when those old fools called the police."

"You don't have to worry on that score. I don't deal with the press."

That wasn't exactly true; I have a great relationship with Lucinda Garcia Mendez, known to her friends as Lucy, a feature reporter with the *Post* who had started following my cases after I'd been involved in the shooting death of a young DC high school student. Her story on that case had been one of the most read articles in the paper when it ran, and she'd been doing them ever since; even going so far as to dub me the Brown Knight, the guy who rides to the rescue of people in need of help who aren't getting it from the system. I had a sense, though, that the good Dr. Winthrop wasn't given to such plebian pursuits as reading a daily newspaper. Hell, he didn't even have a TV in his office. My assumption was right; he nodded, and his thin lips, which had been tense from the beginning of our conversation, relaxed. "Very well, then. I'll cooperate with you. What do you want to know?"

"Well, for starters; you're right; I don't know a thing about medicine, so you'll have to educate me. How could you know she had a stroke or heart attack and not something else?"

Playing to his ego was working; his whole body relaxed as he leaned forward, resting his chin on his fingertips.

"Well, it can sometimes be difficult to diagnose, especially in women. The symptoms of heart problems often present differently than they do in men. But, the patient came to see me around seven in the evening, complaining of heartburn and chest pains. At first, given her terrible dietary habits, I assumed that in fact all she had was a bad case of indigestion. She ate fried food at almost every meal. But, when I examined her, there were other signs that worried me. Her heart rate and blood pressure were elevated, and she complained of pain in both arms and her jaw, blurred vision, and of being extremely tired. I had her lie down and was just about to do an ECG, when she had a seizure."

"You mean a heart attack?"

"If I'd meant a heart attack, I would have said so. She was having a seizure. I didn't suspect a heart attack at first, you must understand. I was preparing the ECG merely as a precaution. When I put the stethoscope to her chest, though, it was clear she was experiencing a cardiac event."

I've never understood doctors and lawyers; they can never say anything in plain English. Why, I wondered, couldn't he just say she was having a heart attack or stroke? A *cardiac event* made it sound like she was some kind of stage performer.

"Okay, she was having an *event*," I tried to keep the sarcasm from my voice, but his narrow-eyed glare told me I'd failed. "What happened then?"

"Well, I tried stimulation, but she suffered a massive stroke at the same time. I used the defibrillator, but it was too little, too late. Between the myocardial infarction and a stroke which severely damaged her brain, there was nothing I could do. She never regained consciousness. Mercifully, the whole thing happened so fast, she probably didn't suffer much."

I wondered if she would have agreed. I've never had either, but I can't imagine having your ticker go crazy on you, and having a blood vessel in your brain pop at the same time, hurts like hell. And, I wished he'd just use plain words – I had to run myocardial infarction through my brain a bit before I realized he was just using a doctor's term for heart attack. Listening to this guy was like trying to follow what they were saying on one of those doctor shows they ran occasionally on NPR; a lot of technical terms that mean nothing to the average person; I sometimes think they do that just to show the rest of us how smart they are, and reaffirm their belief that they know best and we should just shut up, listen, and do what they tell us to do. Thanks, but no thanks.

"So, you called it a heart attack, signed the death certificate, and that was that. Were there any other witnesses?"

"I resent your tone, but basically, yes; that's what I did. It's routine procedure unless there are other factors involved, which in this case there weren't. She was an elderly patient in bad health, and her heart gave out. As to witnesses, I never examine female patients without my nurse being present. I assume you'll want to talk to her?"

"Of course; and, anyone else who might know anything about Geraldine Wallace."

It was beginning to look like I'd gotten all from him that he was willing to give, and my patience was wearing thin; which was just as well, because I'd pissed him off again.

"You can check with the receptionist outside. My nurse's name is Wilomena Dunn. She's probably in the clinic; it's at the back of the building. You can get directions. The general manager of the center is Teresa Arden; her office is near the clinic. As to talking to the residents who might have known her, that's a matter between you and them."

The damned popinjay was casually dismissing me, as if I was an errant schoolboy who'd just been on the receiving end of a lecture by the principal and was being sent back to class. As I left his office, I was wishing his pen would spring a leak and ruin the expensive pearl gray shirt he was wearing.

I found the nurse, a tiny redheaded woman with her hair pulled back from her narrow freckled-dusted face in a ponytail held in place by a pink barrette. She looked to be in her late twenties. Like the doctor, she was wearing a two-piece outfit, called scrubs, but hers were a faded pink color, and she had a stethoscope around her thin neck. Her office was a tiny cubicle with a small metal desk, a metal folding chair which she sat in, and another metal chair beside the desk. She was reading the papers in a brown folder, which she quickly closed when I walked in.

She looked up at me, her dark blue eyes wide as if I'd surprised her. "Yes, may I help you?" She spoke without moving her lips much.

I showed my ID and introduced myself.

"I've just spoken to Dr. Winthrop," I said. "And, he suggested I also talk to you." I gave her the abbreviated version of why I was there. "You were with him when Geraldine Wallace died?"

She bobbed her head up and down. "Uh-huh; the doctor always has me in when he's seeing female patients; not that it matters with most of these old ladies, but he's a stickler about such things."

I sat in the chair next to her desk. It made a creaking sound as I lowered my body gingerly. She winced at the sound.

"What can you tell me about that night?"

"There's not much to tell really. She came in complaining of chest pains, she had a heart attack, and died."

She used simple words, and came straight to the point, but it didn't tell me much.

"How can you be sure it was a heart attack?"

"I haven't been a nurse all that long, but I've seen heart attacks before, and that's what it looked like. Dr. Winthrop tried to revive her, but it all happened so fast. He tried defibbing her for almost ten minutes, but she didn't respond. Look, she was old, ninety I think; and, she had horrible eating habits, lots of grease and fried food; plus, she drank and smoked. That's a good way for a younger, healthier person to have heart trouble. Frankly, I'm surprised she hadn't had problems before."

"She hadn't had heart problems before that night?"

She laid a skinny finger against her thin nose. "Well, er, no; at least none that I know of.

She hadn't been in the clinic before."

"You're telling me that a woman who hadn't been seen by the doctor before just suddenly ups and has a heart attack and dies? Is that normal? Surely she'd had a cold or something before this."

She got up and went to a three-drawer cabinet behind her. Opening it, she withdrew a brown folder. She sat back down and opened the folder, which contained a single sheet held in place by clasps.

"See, here in her file," she said. "She only came to the clinic once; her first and unfortunately, last time. She never even got shots. We recommend the elderly get flu shots every year and shots for shingles if they ever had chicken pox, but she never did."

"Okay, I get your point; but, cremating her right away bothers me. Why did you do that?"

She shrugged. "Hey, you have to ask Terry; that's Teresa Alden, our general manager; about that. It wasn't our decision to do, it was hers."

"Where can I find this Teresa Alden?"

"You might try turning around," a voice said from behind me. "Winthrop called me and said you'd be looking for me. Let's go into my office."

I turned and looked up at the source of the voice. I didn't feel like not complying.

Chapter 4

Teresa Arden wasn't big in a bulky sense, but she was nonetheless imposing.

She was tall; probably half an inch taller than my six feet; with broad but not manly shoulders, a narrow waist that flared out into generous hips, long legs, with muscular calves that I could see beneath the short brown skirt she wore that showed a large expanse of thigh. She wore a beige blouse that jutted out in front, removing any doubt that, her size notwithstanding, she was definitely of the female persuasion. She had a square jaw and wore the minimum of makeup; dark brown eyes looked down at me impassively.

I rose and extended my hand. Her grip was firm.

"Ms. Arden," I said. "I do need to ask you a few questions. Is there somewhere private we can speak privately?"

Her expression was cold and unyielding. "Why should I speak to you about anything?"

"Well, Dr. Winthrop and Nurse Dunn here have already spoken to me. Why would you be hesitant to do so?"

She looked down at Wilomena Dunn, who had shrunk into her chair, looking completely cowed. "I just don't see how the affairs of our residents should be any of our business. What the doctor and Willie here do regarding medical matters is different; although, I have my concerns even about that; but, the other affairs of people in residence here is not for public discussion. We value their privacy."

"Geraldine Wallace is dead, I might remind you. I hardly think she's in a position to complain about her privacy being invaded."

I said it with a smile on my face. She didn't appreciate the humor. "Be that as it may, I don't see how they should concern you. Morgan said you were asking questions about how she died. That's a medical issue; what does it have to do with her business affairs?"

"Maybe nothing, maybe everything," I said. "I understand you were the one who had her immediately cremated. In some minds that might look suspicious if someone thought maybe she didn't really die of natural causes. If you've nothing to hide, why wouldn't you want to talk to me about it?"

Her right eyebrow arched upwards. She glared down at the nurse who seemed to be trying to make herself even smaller or disappear into the wall. "Uh, maybe we should talk in my office." She turned and walked off without even waiting to see if I was following.

Of course, I was following; right close behind her.

Her office was two doors down from the nurse's, next to a door marked clinic. She walked in and when I'd entered behind her, she closed the door and went to her desk. She sat down, motioning me to a cushioned chair at the side. Her office wasn't quite as fancy as the doctor's; she wasn't given to displays of art or certificates, but it was still well appointed. A large desk dominated the room, and the chair behind it, in which she sat, was one of those high-backed executive chairs with arms and covered in what looked like real leather. She had a laptop computer and a phone with more buttons than the receptionist's. Next to the phone was a box with twelve numbered buttons. Two TV monitors sat in a case to her left; one was tuned to a cable news channel, while the other showed the reception area. So, she kept tabs on the place, probably with the box of buttons.

"Okay, Mr. Pennyback; what do you want to know?"

"Why don't we start with why you cremated Wallace so quickly after she died? Shouldn't you have tried to contact next of kin for instructions first?"

"You go right for the jugular, don't you? We cremated her because that was her wish; it's in her contract that was signed when she took up residence here. As to why it was done so quickly; what was the point in waiting? She had no next of kin to consult, and it seemed ghoulish to just let her body lie in our cooler."

"So, since she has no next of kin, how did you dispose of her estate?"

She looked at me now like I was something a dog had left on the carpet. Okay, so I do go for the jugular. The more I talked to people, the more things just smelled off. I couldn't say what was bothering me, but my antenna were out and buzzing.

"She didn't have much; a few thousand in the bank, and some jewelry, clothing, and a few odds and ends. We gave her clothing to Goodwill; the rest goes to the center."

"The center's a few thousand dollars richer with her passing. Is that normal, I mean, when residents die, they leave everything to this place?"

"Not all of them, no; some have relatives, and if they leave their estate to the next of kin, that's who gets it. Others, like Geraldine Wallace, who have no family, usually make bequests to the center. You could say it's their way of expressing their gratitude for us for taking care of them in their declining years. We're a full-service assisted living facility. Look, Mr. Pennyback; the elderly, often even those with relatives, tend to be sidelined. They appreciate the attention we give them. There's nothing out of the ordinary about it. Would you prefer they left everything to a house full of cats?"

I'm allergic to cats, and they know it, so our feline friends wouldn't be surprised to know I'm not a fan of them being the sole heirs of some poor person's estate. I wasn't about to tell Teresa Arden that, though.

"Are you suggesting that we somehow did something wrong in this case?" she asked. Her eyes blazed. "Because, if you are, I assure you, I'd have our lawyers file a defamation suit in a heartbeat. We have a reputation to protect, and I'm not about to sit idly by and have someone smear it on the basis of some wild-ass allegation."

That sounded very much like a threat, and I don't like being threatened. "I assure you, Ms. Arden; I have no desire to smear anyone. I've been hired, though, to look into this, and I owe it to *my* clients to give it my best shot. That means asking questions that might make you uncomfortable. If I do that, believe me, it's not personal. If you have nothing to hide, you have nothing to fear from me."

"I just want to be clear on where we stand. You go ahead and ask your questions, but if you start spreading rumors, it won't be me who has to fear. I'll have your license pulled if you step out of line."

She was threatening me; blatantly. I was beginning to dislike her. At the same time, it didn't make sense to push it too far until I had something to push with. "I get your message. I'm not trying to start trouble. Hell, it's probably as routine as you've said. But, you have some residents who have questions. Don't you think it's a good idea to put their minds at rest on this issue? I mean, we're both professionals with a job to do. In this case, I think our interests converge. You want to maintain the reputation and standards of your center, and I want to help a few old people feel secure. Seems to me, instead of going at each other's throats, we should be working together; that way, we both get what we want."

I had her pegged as an officious bully, and there's two ways to handle bullies; you can punch them between the eyes, but when you do that, you can no longer get their cooperation; or, you can play to their ego; let them think they have the upper hand. I decided to take the second course, and it seemed to be working. She smiled slightly, a self-satisfied look like a cat with a bowl full of milk and a side order of canary.

"You have a point," she said. "I guess I'm just a little sensitive when it comes to our reputation. Okay, you have my full cooperation. Is there anything else you'd like to know?"

When she smiled and stopped trying to play the female version of Attila the Hun, she wasn't unattractive. Not my type, but I could see where she'd be considered a catch by some men. Not that I'd turn my back on her.

"I can't think of anything at the moment. But, I hope I can call you if I think of something else. The quicker I can get some kind of credible answer to my clients the better for both of us, right?"

"Of course. Can you tell me who your clients are?" There was that stalking cat expression again.

"You'll understand that client confidentiality is important in my business."

"That's all right; I know it has to be that troublemaker Bill Powderly and his little crew. That man's been nothing but trouble since the day he came here. Questions everything, and is forever breaking center rules. Don't worry, though, he and his little friends won't hear from me that I know about them."

I wasn't surprised that she knew. The place wasn't that large, and the receptionist had probably already told her I'd met Powderly. In addition, I figured she had a camera somewhere that enabled her to see my meeting with him and his friends. She was slick, though. Not even one indication that it was anything more than a keen insight on her part. I'd have to tread carefully with this one. I decided to continue to play her little game. "Thanks for that. Wouldn't do for them to think I went around blabbing about them."

The sound of her door slamming open startled us both. She looked up with a frown that quickly morphed into a feline smile. "Burton, what are you doing here?"

A burly character, square jawed with a blond buzz cut and ears that looked like a pink version of Dumbo's, stood in the doorway, frowning down at me. He was wearing faded jeans that bulged over his well-developed thighs, and a dark blue work shirt. His large hands were tanned and scuffed.

"Hey, babe," he said. "I got off work today; the union called a strike; so, I thought I'd come see if you wanted to grab lunch with me. Who's your friend?"

She hesitated, looking from me to him. "Uh,

this is Mr. Pennyback. He's doing some work for us."

He continued to scowl at me. "Looks like a cop to me. What kind of work would a cop be doing for an old folks' home?"

"Burton, I've told you, this is not an old folks' home; it's an assisted living facility. And, Mr. Pennyback is not a policeman."

I had just about to introduce myself, but for some reason, she didn't seem to want to tell him who and what I was, so I just played along and kept my mouth shut.

"You ain't a cop, eh? What are you then?"

Teresa Arden looked, talked and dressed like a well-educated woman. This guy came across as definitely low-brow, and the jealous type to boot. I'm not fond of deceiving people unless it's instrumental to my inquiries, but she saved me from having to come up with a cover story.

"Mr. Pennyback is a researcher, and he's doing some research for us," she said. "Mr. Pennyback, this is Burton Linde; he's my, uh, close friend."

He laughed. "Oh yeah, I'm her *friend*. That means I'm her boyfriend. What's the matter, babe, shamed of me? What kinda research do you do, Pennyback?"

"I'm afraid that's a little sensitive." She

turned to me. "Thank you for stopping in, Mr. Pennyback. We'll be in touch."

She rose and extended her hand. I could feel a slight tremor as I shook it.

"Thanks," I said. "I'll keep you advised of my . . . research."

As I squeezed past Linde, he continued to glare at me; puffing out his chest to demonstrate his alpha-maleness. I simply nodded and left, pulling the door closed behind me.

Making my way back to the parking lot, I was thinking I'd like to be a fly on the wall at that moment in Teresa Arden's office.

Chapter 5

On my way into the District, I swung by a KFC and picked up a two-piece chicken meal. By the time I got to the office, the bag they'd put it in was dark with grease.

Heather wrinkled her nose when I walked in.

"Yeew," she said. "You're eating fried for lunch again, aren't you?"

"Didn't have time to stop at Mom's, so I thought I'd eat at my desk."

"Well, hurry up and take it to your own office. That fried chicken smell is apt to get in my hair and take forever to shampoo out."

Heather never eats fried anything. Me; on the other hand; I like fried food. A remnant of my Texas upbringing, when if it wasn't fried, it was dessert, and even then sometimes, it was fried. She eats healthy things like bean sprouts and unidentifiable things made from soy cake, and washes them down with herbal tea. I eat healthy sometimes, especially when I eat with Sandra, but when I'm rushed, fried is the way to go.

"Okay, I'll open the window so the place can air out. Look, I went to see your friends at the retirement center. You'll be happy to know I'm taking their case; so, you need to draw up a contract. We can take it out to get a signature on Monday sometime. After I finish my lunch I'll fill you in so you can start a case file."

"Fine, just get that stuff out of smell range, will you."

I'd stuffed several paper napkins into the bag when I bought it, but by the time I got to my desk, they were soggy, so I had to wipe the grease from my face with my fingers, which earned me more glares from Heather when I had to pass her desk to get to the john to wash my hands. It was the better part of an hour of scrubbing with the jasmine-scented hand soap she buys before she pronounced me toxin-free and would allow me to sit near her desk to brief her on the case. I kept my hands in my lap. The smell of the chicken grease was preferable to the back room at a funeral parlor smell of the soap.

"Okay," I said. "Now that I smell like a flower

shop, are you ready to get to work on this case?"

She took a deep breath, and smiled. "Now, that's so much better. You smell human at last." She couldn't resist rubbing it in. "Okay, shoot; what did you think of the old folks?"

I gave her a rundown of the suspicions Powderly and his friends had about the death of their friend, and recapped my conversations with the three center employees. I didn't say anything about my concerns, especially my unease at being around the elderly. Heather's the soul of discretion, but she's also very sensitive about some things; not just greasy odors; and she might take it the wrong way.

"Do you think they're imagining things?" she asked when I finished. "Could it be that their friend just died of natural causes?"

"Sure, it could be. But, there's just enough off about this to make me wonder. Anyway, I'll dig into it; if nothing else, finding out that she did die of natural causes should ease their minds."

She smiled. My assault on her tender sense of smell was forgiven.

Chapter 6

The next morning, Saturday, dawned brightly; and I was up before the sun.

I pulled on an old sweat and a pair of scruffy running shoes and prodded Sandra, who was still curled up under the sheet.

"Okay, sleepy head; time to stretch those beautiful muscles of yours."

"Gwayne lemlun," her muffled voice came from beneath the squirming sheet. "lemsleep."

I poked the beautiful round hump that was one of her luscious hips, causing her to scoot away from my finger. Finally, her head, with her blonde tresses all over the place, poked from beneath the sheet. "Okay, if you're not going to go away and let me sleep, I guess I'll have to get up," she said, stifling a yawn. "But, I'll have you know I consider this abuse of the worse kind."

She had a good excuse for not wanting to get up. The previous evening, I'd decided to celebrate it being Friday by taking her to a Chinese restaurant in Gaithersburg that specialized in Sichuan cuisine. The spicy dishes they serve had to be washed down with large quantities of imported Chinese beer that came in liter bottles, and we'd had two each. We got home around half past ten, and had a couple of Mexican beers before tumbling into the sack and playing around for an hour or so before getting up, showering and then getting in bed to sleep. I felt a little wrung out, but my years in the army had taught me that when you're tired in the morning, nothing wakes you up like a vigorous run, followed by more vigorous exercise and a big breakfast.

I hadn't quite convinced Sandra that this made sense, but she humored me. She rolled off the bed. She was wearing nothing but a skimpy pair of panties that revealed more than concealed her treasures. Even half asleep, with her hair drooping over her half-lidded eyes, she's one of the most beautiful women I've ever seen. The fact that she never tries to flaunt her looks makes her even more beautiful.

She padded to the closet and pulled out her own sweats and sneakers.

"I'll get us two waters," I said. "Meet you out back."

She was pulling a sweatshirt over her head, so whatever she said in reply was muffled, which was probably just as well, because it was probably an unflattering description of my ancestry.

I was waiting on the back porch of the farmhouse that we now more or less shared – even though she kept her little cozy place in Takoma Park, she'd moved a lot of her things into my, our, place – when she came through the door. Her sweats failed to conceal that she had a very athletic and appealing figure. Awake now, her cheeks flushed and still damp from the cold water I know she'd used to wake herself up, she didn't look too angry at being roused out of bed.

"Okay; I guess I'm as ready as I'll ever be."

We did a few stretches to loosen up our muscles, and then set off at an easy jog over the uneven ground of my backyard, quickly entering the forest of scattered pines, oaks and chestnuts in back. As we hit the area that started sloping down toward the C&O Canal and the Potomac River, we picked up the pace. She easily matched my pace, and even after fifteen minutes wasn't breathing very hard.

By the time we'd made the turn at about three miles, and headed back uphill toward the house, she'd gotten into the spirit of things, and challenged me to a sprint as we neared the edge of the trees. I beat her by only a few feet, but my lungs were paying for the effort it took. She laughed and slapped my back as she pulled up beside me.

"Not bad for an old man. Next time, though, I'm gonna leave you eating my dust. Are we going to work out on the big bag?"

She was fully awake now. We walked together to the old barn where I keep some free weights and an old punching bag I'd scored from a gym near my office that was closing down from lack of patrons. I'd offered the owner money, but he said the bag was ready for the junk pile anyway, so I was just saving him from having to take it down and lug it out behind the building.

We did twenty minutes of punching and kicking; Sandra was getting really proficient at Karate, which I'd been teaching her. I could take her still, but she made me work for it. Pity the man or woman who tried mugging her.

Back in the house, we stripped and showered together, horsing around and splashing water all over the bathroom. After toweling off and dressing, her in a blue tee shirt and white shorts, me in a sleeveless sweater and faded jeans, we went to the kitchen to prepare our Saturday breakfast.

Breakfast consisted of buttermilk pancakes and hash browns, cooked by me, with sausages and scrambled eggs whipped up by Sandra. I'd beaten her to the kitchen and started a pot of freshly ground Colombian coffee brewing; the rich aroma permeated the entire kitchen. We'd gotten weekend breakfast preparation down to a smoothly choreographed routine, with little bumping into each other as we moved from sink to stove to table, and that was deliberate. If you'd ever seen Sandra in tee shirt and shorts you'd understand why that would happen.

After a run, exercise and a hot shower, she was her normal cheerful self, and had completely forgiven me for dragging her out of bed before the sun's rays were even coming through the gap in the bedroom window curtains.

"I hate to admit it," she said, leaning over to give me a light kiss on my unshaven cheek. "But, getting up early and exercising to get the muscles loose and the blood pumping isn't such a bad idea. I feel positively energized."

I rubbed my cheek against hers, causing her to flinch, and then patted her on a well-rounded nether cheek. "Getting a good start makes the whole day go better. That includes a good meal." Seven days a week, I got up around the same time, and basically did the same things, even when all I planned to do was crawl back in bed. "It's a good idea to have a routine; keeps your mind on track and sharp."

"You sound like some kind of Zen master."

"More like a drill sergeant. When I was a kid, I worked on this old man's farm during school vacations, and he never took a holiday. Used to say, hens and cows don't have a calendar. Cows need milking every day, and the eggs got to be gathered. Then, I joined the army, and the drill sergeants didn't only ignore holidays; for them, day and night were all the same. They're philosophy was, if you're in combat, you don't take time outs or holidays, so you had to train your body and mind for that. Guess it's just stuck with me."

"I don't plan on going to war, and I'll get my eggs and milk from the supermarket, thank you; but, I do feel good, and I'm hungry enough to eat a whole cow."

"Afraid you'll have to settle for flapjacks and potatoes, princess."

I put four-high stacks of the golden brown pancakes on two plates, with two hash brown patties beside each stack, and then put the plates on the little table in the breakfast nook just off the kitchen. While Sandra ladled sausages and eggs on the plates, I poured two mugs of coffee and put them beside the plates. A container of maple syrup that I keep in the cupboard, and bottles of hot sauce and catsup, completed our breakfast table. The smell of sausage, maple syrup and freshly done pancakes mixed with the aroma of the coffee, reminding me of the way my grandmother's kitchen smelled when I was a kid.

I'm not one for talking during breakfast; or any other meal for that matter, although Buster Mayweather and I sometimes discuss cases over soul food at Mom's on Sixteenth Street, but that's another matter; and, Sandra, after having lived with me for so long, has become the same. We dug into our food, the only noises our sighs of satisfaction and the clinking sound of silverware against the plates.

We both cleaned our plates, and I poured us second cups of coffee which we took into the living room. We sat on the sofa; our feet propped on the coffee table, and listened to big band music on an NPR morning show on the radio, sipping our coffee.

"One more week of school, and I can finally rest," Sandra said. "This has, for some reason, been one of our busiest school years."

"How'd you like to take a trip this summer?" I asked.

"Really; where did you have in mind?" Her eyes were wide and she was smiling like a kid about to open her birthday present.

"I hadn't given it much thought. Where would you like to go?"

She laid a slender finger against her aquiline

nose and tilted her head.

"I've never been to Texas, and I've always wanted to see the state that shaped you into the person you are." She had an impish look on her face.

Sandra knows well that, while I love my home state, it's more an abstract romanticism than any desire to ever go back. With my parents having been swept away by a hurricane when they were visiting an aunt at her beachside house near Galveston, leaving not even bodies to bury or grave sites to visit, I have no real relatives left there. Oh, a few distant cousins here and there, but, in Texas everyone's someone else's cousin. Most of them, I couldn't even remember their names, including one who'd left me several acres of forest land north of Houston, the management of which I'd turned over to his two sons and an old Indian man who lived there. So, I couldn't believe she was seriously suggesting we take our vacation there.

"I don't think your first visit to the Lone Star State should be in summer," I said. "Especially not East Texas where I grew up."

"What's the matter, babe, are you ashamed of your home town?"

I laughed; a barking sound. "Ashamed of it? I don't think of it enough to be ashamed of it. But, sweetheart, East Texas in summer is like being locked in a steam bath. Temperatures soar to triple digits and hang there for weeks, and the humidity is like being wrapped in a wet wool blanket. Oh, and the bugs are as big as birds. Trust me, you would not enjoy it."

"You sound like a typical Texan; birds as big as bats my eye. Surely you exaggerate."

I gave her one of my most serious looks. "Babe, when it comes to mosquitos and horseflies in Texas, there's no need to exaggerate. They truly are *big*. I'll take you there next winter; when it's cold here, it's only mildly cool there, and I think you'd like it. I was thinking this summer we'd go somewhere more romantic."

"Romantic? Umm, I like the sound of that. Maybe the Caribbean?"

"Now you're talking. Blue skies and white sand beaches; sitting on hammocks and sipping rum punch. You're on. As soon as school is out, and I finish the current case I'm working on, we're off."

"What's your current case? Something icky and dangerous, I bet."

I filled her in on my probing of Geraldine Wallace's demise, giving her my take on the people I'd spoken to. When I finished, she leaned her head against my shoulder and patted my thigh.

"Do you think there's anything to their suspicions? I mean, the lady who died was ninety after all."

"I don't know. My lizard brain's telling me something smells about the whole thing; but, that could be from my reaction to Winthrop and Arden. Those two are the worse kind of bureaucrats; the people in that place are just numbers on a piece of paper to them. The nurse seemed a good enough sort, but who knows."

"It's terrible the way the elderly are treated. They work and take care of their kids for decades, and then, when they get old they're shipped off to an institution and forgotten."

"My three clients aren't the type to sit quietly and be ignored, that's for sure. I got the sense they're real burrs under the saddles of the doctor and the director."

"You and your impossible cases," she said, punching me lightly in the ribs. "How are you going to prove anything one way or another without a body?"

Leave it to her to zero in on the main problem; without a body or an independently conducted medical examination, I only had my clients' suspicions and allegations. Unless I could find some evidence of wrongdoing on the part of Winthrop or one of the others, I was spitting in a hurricane. Of course, that didn't mean I wouldn't try.

"Guess I'll just have to do it the old fashioned way; keep digging and asking questions; turn over enough rocks until something crawls out."

"Well, at least this one isn't as dangerous as most of your cases."

"There is that."

"Don't you feel guilty, though; taking money from old people who must be living on fixed incomes?"

"These guys aren't poor, babe. Getting into Shady Grove is like getting admitted to an exclusive prep school. I'll bet there's a waiting list. I don't think there'll be much in the way of expenses, so they're only paying my daily fee, and, if it'll make you feel better, I won't charge them for weekends."

"You, my sweet, have a heart of gold."

"Don't I deserve a reward for my goodness?"

"What did you have in mind?"

I pulled her against me, nibbling gently at the base of her neck, and letting my hand trail softly up her smooth thigh.

"Oh, that," she said.

Chapter 7

We spent the rest of Saturday in bed, skipping lunch and only getting out to eat a light supper.

We'd promised my friend Carlton Raine that we'd join him and his lady love, Elizabeth Sung, for Sunday brunch, so we rolled out of bed at six, exercised, showered, and napped until nine, when we got up, dressed and drove to his place.

Carlton lives in a cabin he built himself, near the town of Poolesville, on a private dirt road on what had once been a farm. He's surrounded by pine forest, but has cut the trees back from around the house, giving him more than a hundred yards of clear area that anyone trying to sneak up on him has to cross. I know he has cameras and listening devices hidden in the woods and along the road, but have never been able to spot them. No one has ever tried to attack his house, and I feel sorry for the first fool that tries. He has a small armory in the metal-lined room behind his living room; enough firepower to hold off a battalion, and he's proficient with every piece.

He's 84, but time has neither rounded his shoulders nor bent his back. There are a few lines on his smooth brown face, and his hair is thinning on top and streaked with gray. But, he still has all his own teeth, and when he shakes your hand, you can feel the strength.

I introduced him to Elizabeth Sung, a Chinese-American lawyer I'd met when a tong member I'd helped put away escaped from prison and came looking for revenge. She's 38, looks 25, and has a healthy libido. Carlton keeps up with her though. After visiting his house for the first two weeks after I introduced them, to help him brush up on his Mandarin, she finally moved in full time.

Carlton was wearing blue pants, a powder blue dress shirt opened at the collar, and a dark blue blazer with brass buttons. Elizabeth wore a dark green one-piece dress that looked like it had been painted on, with a slit from ankle to well up her bronzed thigh on the right side. Fortunately, knowing Carlton's somewhat old-fashioned ways, I knew the two of them would dress for the occasion, so Sandra and I had put on what we thought was our Sunday best; dark brown slacks and a blue shirt with a light tan jacket for me, a blue pantsuit that set off her athletic figure for her. Thankfully, Sandra and Elizabeth got along, so there wasn't any of the jostling and jockeying women getup to sometimes over who looked best; they both looked great and knew it, so they felt no need to compete.

As usual, Carlton had been standing in the door of his cabin, Elizabeth at his side, as my Mustang negotiated the final curve in the dirt track leading from River Road. I'd craned my neck throughout the drive, as I always did, trying to spot the cameras, again with no luck.

He took my hand in a firm grip as I mounted the steps. Sandra and Elizabeth embraced, kissing each other on the cheek; none of that pecking at the air crap for them. I hugged Elizabeth as Carlton bowed and kissed Sandra's hand. She blushed. Old guy still had a way with women.

"Come on in, you two," he said. "Liz has been working all morning to get things ready for you."

Elizabeth smiled and took his arm as we entered the cabin.

"He's exaggerating," she said. "He did as much work as I did."

And, she was probably right. The living room

was much as I'd always seen it; a large sofa set in the middle with a low table in front, end tables with low lamps at each end, and two cushioned chairs at each end of the table; everything set well away from the walls, giving room for someone familiar with the layout to move about easily. Two silver trays, laden with pate-covered crackers and little wedges of cheese and pearl onions, with a bottle of red wine and four fluted glasses next to them, sat in the center of the table. The smell of baked ham and sweet potato pie drifted in from the kitchen just off to the left of the living room. Directly opposite the entrance door, a three-inch thick, metal lined monstrosity that swung easily on recessed hinges was a larger door that looked even more formidable. I knew that behind that door he had a state-of-the-art computer and surveillance system and a metal locker containing an array of weapons and ammunition, along with other high-tech gizmos that Carlton's former colleagues at the agency often 'loaned' him for testing. Most of the devices weren't anything you'd ever read about, or even suspect the existence of. He'd once shared one with me; probably breaking every regulation in the book by doing so; but, then, Carlton 'Blood' Raine and I had a special relationship. He was the closest thing to a father I'd had since my own father died.

"You two make yourselves at home," he said, pouring wine into four glasses as he spoke. He passed the filled glasses around, first to Sandra, then Elizabeth, and finally me. He then lifted his own. "Here's to good friends."

Ever the gentleman, Carlton ushered the two women to the sofa, nodding at me to take the chair on the left, while he sat opposite me in the other chair.

"It's been a while since you visited us, young man," he said. "I'd be upset that you keep this lovely lady away from me, if I didn't have Liz here to enjoy gazing upon. What have you been up to?"

He has that soft, slightly drawling southern way of talking that you like listening to, like some old professor gently chiding wayward students.

"I don't really have an excuse. The time just slips by before you know it."

"Is that another way of saying that you've not had any cases recently that are too obtuse for that sharp mind of yours to penetrate?"

"Aw, come on, Blood, you know that's not the only reason I visit you." Well, at least, not the main reason. I did tend to seek him out when I've run into that brick wall the second or third time; he has a way of seeing past the fog and getting to the truth of a thing like no one I've ever known. I also liked his company, my unease around most old people notwithstanding.

"Actually, I have a case right now that falls into that category," I said.

"See, I told you," he said, winking at Elizabeth. "Boy only comes out here when he's got a problem."

"Oh, Carlton, give him a break," she said, smiling back at him. "He means well. You know how youngsters can be."

They were having fun at my expense, and Sandra was enjoying seeing me squirm, which was really funny, given that Elizabeth a decade younger than me. I guess that comes from hanging around someone like Blood Raine.

"For your information," I said with feigned indignation. "I'd accepted this invitation before I took my present case, so there."

"Likely story," Carlton said. "Is that true, Sandra dear?"

Sandra looked at me with a Cheshire cat smile, her head cocked to the side, and a twinkle in her eyes. I tensed. The ribbing wasn't over. Damn!

"Actually, it is," she said after a long pause. "He just took the case on Friday."

"Well, in that case, I guess I'll have to let you off the hook. What's this case that's giving you so much trouble?"

I went over the case, with complete descriptions of my conversations. Carlton has the ability to listen so intently when you're speaking to him you get the feeling he's peering right into your brain and knows what you're about to say a microsecond before you say it.

"So, you have three oldsters claiming their friend didn't die of natural causes, but no corpus to prove or disprove it, and no solid evidence to indicate foul play, right?" he said after I'd finished.

"That's about it."

"That's a problem, all right."

"Any suggestions?"

He nibbled on the knuckle of his right index finger, looking down at the floor. That was a sign of deep thought on his part.

"That is a puzzler, all right," he said. "I assume you're planning to do a full background check on the deceased?"

"Yeah; especially to see if she ever had any kind of medical condition."

"Don't forget while you're at it to check the value of her estate carefully." I nodded; I'd thought of that. "The next thing you might want to do is see if there's a history of this at the center."

My brows raised in puzzlement. "A history of what?" I asked.

"Elderly people with no next of kin and healthy estates suddenly kicking the bucket. If there's anything untoward going on, this isn't likely to be the first time."

Like I said, Carlton gets to the point of an issue quicker than anyone I know. I'm pretty good at puzzles myself, but I hadn't thought about looking into the history and background of the place in relation to my current case. I made a mental note to get Heather working on it first thing. It still left me with the task of proving wrongdoing in Geraldine Wallace's case, but if there were any skeletons in Shady Grove's closets, it might give me something to pressure them with.

"Good idea, Blood; I hadn't thought of that. What I know about medicine you could stick in your eye and it wouldn't itch. Of course, I still can't prove conclusively that she didn't die of a heart attack because there was no autopsy, and since she's been cremated, I can't finagle one. Hell, is it even legal for them to do that?"

"You mean dispose of the body without an autopsy? It depends. If it was her wish to be cremated, they're covered there, and, as for the autopsy, in a case where there was a doctor in attendance and he certified the cause of death, unless there's evidence of some other crime, it's not usually required. Even in suspicious cases, because of religious restrictions, it's sometimes hard to get a regular autopsy done."

"How did an agency guy come by such knowledge? I thought you spent most of your career working overseas."

He chuckled. "Well, according to the rules, I was only legally allowed to ply my trade outside the borders of the country . . . but, you have to remember, I was active in the agency during the height of the Cold War. The KGB and their thugs didn't have any qualms about operating on U.S. soil, and sometimes we had to bend the rules to thwart their activities."

"I'm not sure I should be hearing this," I said. I glanced over at Sandra and Elizabeth who had their heads together talking and seemed to be ignoring us. "Deniability, you know."

"Hell, boy; you were in special operations. You know you guys didn't always play by the rules. If you had, you'd have been dead more than likely; at best, the bad guys would have run rings around you."

I thought about my old friend, Tony Park, and his outfit, the successor to the old team I once commanded, and his sudden appearance in DC when I was trying to help a woman find out what had happened to her fiancé. During my investigation, I'd gotten involved with the African immigrant community, and it turned out that a terrorist organization was using it as a cover for fund raising and plans for operations against us. Tony and his guys had come out of nowhere, taken the bad guys down, and faded back into the woodwork like wisps of fog in a forest, killing one and taking the other into custody. I never knew what happened; there was no press coverage, and the local police hadn't even asked me about the incident. Yes, Blood was right; in the fight against people who honor no rules, the side that tries to play strictly according to the book is likely to come out on the low side. On the other hand, though, I'd learned during my years in the army that rules are necessary. Without limits, government organizations, any organizations, can become tools of repression as bad as the ones they claim to be defending against.

I didn't say any of that to Blood. He'd come from a different era; a time when citizens were spied on, experimented on, all in the name of national security. I'd gotten out of it after an operation turned into a tragedy because of faulty intelligence, and had no desire to return to it.

"I always tried to follow the rules," I said. "They're there for a purpose. If we violate them, we're no better than the other guy." That was as close as I'd come to rebuking him. The jibe hit home. He frowned and looked pensively at the floor.

"You have a point. I'm not proud of some of the things I did. But, at the time, I thought I had no other choice. You have to remember, not only were we facing enemies who made their own rules; not as bad as these suicide bombers who're making such a fuss over in the Middle East now; but, bad enough, but, as one of the first black field operatives in the agency, I had to be meaner, faster, smarter, and deadlier than everyone else just to be considered acceptable."

His story of being a minority in an agency that until that time had been mostly lily white and male had come out bit by bit during our few meetings. I didn't envy what he'd gone through. It's always hard being the 'first.' Like Henry O. Flipper, the first black to graduate from West Point, he'd endured periods when no one else would speak to him, or even sit in the same lunch room with him. Unlike Flipper, who'd been wrongfully accused of theft and railroaded out of the army, Carlton 'Blood' Raine had proven himself to be, not just as good as, but a hell of a lot better, than those who shunned him, eventually becoming a station chief at a small embassy in Africa, one of the first non-whites to achieve that status, and earned the respect, sometimes grudging, of his colleagues. When he retired just before he turned 65, he was one of the most respected members of the secretive Directorate of Operations, and was frequently consulted by the younger officers who'd heard tales of his exploits during their orientation at The Farm, and who just wanted to be near the legendary 'Blood.'

I knew how they felt. The man radiated competence, and, even in his eighties, had an air of danger about him that was palpable.

I simply nodded in acknowledgement. There was no need for words; there were no words to express what we both understood.

He shook himself, breaking the somber mood that his words had created.

"Hell fire, where are my manners. You folks must be famished. Why don't we eat, eh? I made my special honey-infused ham and a sweet potato pie that will melt in your mouth."

He stood and moved toward the kitchen. Elizabeth pulled away from Sandra and stood, placing her shapely hands on his shoulders.

"You just sit down," she said. "Sandra and I will serve the food. Besides, the way you two were huddling, you must have more to talk about."

He gave me a look; there was something in his gaze that told me that my reaction to his description of his activities in the agency had changed our relationship. The question was, for the better or for the worse?

"I guess we do at that," he said. He sat, with his legs crossed and his hands on his knees. "So, you think we should always take the moral high ground when we face an enemy, no matter how he behaves, do you?"

He was nothing if not blunt – getting right to the point; that was Blood's strong suit. It was one of the things, among many, that I really liked about the man.

"Yes, I do believe it," I said. "I know it's not always possible. Humans make mistakes; but, we should strive to always do what's right. That's the only thing that separates us from the bad guys."

"Let me give you a hypothetical situation then. What if some group attacked this country, like the Japanese attack on Pearl Harbor in 1941; without warning; would you follow the rules in retaliating?"

"I'm assuming you're talking about something other than a conventional military attack?" Everyone knows how we responded during the Second World War; it ended with Japan being the only country on the planet to suffer not one, but two atomic attacks. "Something like an attack by a terrorist group?"

"Precisely; and, before you say that's impossible, don't forget, there's already been an attempt to bomb the World Trade Center in New York back in 1993. A lot of people looked at that as just a one-off operation by a bunch of crackpots; but, it's actually a warning signal. There are a lot of groups out there, some of them not part of any national structure, that would like to bring us down, and they don't operate by any civilized code of conduct you or I would recognize. If we were attacked by someone like that, would you insist we abide by the rules in fighting them?"

"Yes, I would. Look, I know what you're getting at; but, if we get down to the level of people like that, in the end they win, not us. I don't doubt what you say, but I don't think it should matter if we're going to war against a country or a terrorist organization; if we don't behave in an ethical way, we forfeit our right to claim moral superiority. Hell, we lose before the fight's even over."

He looked intently at me; as if he was looking through me. Then, he laughed; a deep, hearty laugh, and slapped his knee. "That's what I like about you, Al; you speak your mind, and you have a first-rate mind. You're absolutely right. What we did during the Cold War in the interest of expediency was sometimes wrong, and counterproductive. Of course, you couldn't have told us that back then. We were young and full of piss and vinegar, and sure that we had God on our side. I can see another situation like that coming, and soon; and, I worry that we won't have enough people around like you. We came out of the abyss during the Cold War; thanks to the collapse of the Soviet Union; but, I think we're on the brink of another even as we speak."

I shook my head. "I think you're getting gloomy in our old age, Blood."

"Maybe, maybe not. I actually hope I'm wrong. Anyway, not much an old fart like me can do about it."

Just then, Elizabeth stuck her head around the corner of the dining nook door. "Food's on guys; come get it while it's hot."

"Food's not the only thing that's hot around here," Carlton said, winking at me.

Chapter 8

"I want you to dig deeply into Shady Grove and the good Dr. Winthrop," I said to Heather the next morning.

I was sitting next to her desk, my note pad in hand, going over the notes I'd made after leaving Blood and Elizabeth to whatever they had planned for after brunch activity the day before.

"What in particular do you want me to look for?"

"See how many of the residents of the place have died for, oh, say, the past four or five years, and under what circumstances. I'm particular interested in those who had no next of kin. As for the doctor, dig deep; I want to know everything about him, from his grades in med school to his favorite hair tonic – oh, forget that, he's bald – what color his underwear is."

"You're planning to tell me what this is all leading to, aren't you?"

"Look; I'm just trying to satisfy our clients. If you dig and find nothing, it probably means the old lady did just have a heart attack, so they can stop fretting. If, on the other hand, you turn up something suspicious, it'll give me leverage to press Winthrop."

"Do you really think it's possible he wrongly certified the cause of death?"

"Right now, I'm not thinking *anything*. But, we don't have a body to examine, so we need to go at this indirectly, get it."

She was making notes on a legal pad; despite being something of a computer genius, she likes to do notes in regular writing now and then – of course, she immediately transfers them to a computer file, which I've always thought of as double work, but then, I rarely do anything on the computer other than read my emails; which I routinely delete as soon as I've read them; and play chess. I've yet to defeat the computer, although I've come close a couple of times. She tapped her pen on the pad and looked up at me, smiling.

"Ah, I get it. Since we can't prove wrongdoing in the current case, we see if there's a history of it. If that's the case, maybe the police can be forced to take the complaint seriously."

"Right; and, even if the cops don't buy it, it would give me something to goad Winthrop with."

"You think he did something bad?"

"Like I said, I'm not prejudging, but he's the doctor. Seems to me he'd be the logical suspect. He's the one who said it was just a heart attack; as a doctor, he ought to know the difference between a heart attack and someone being done it, right?"

She gave me a squinty eye look. "How would you expect me to know? I know computers, not people; and, speaking of people, you want me to run checks on everyone else at the center, of course."

"Of course; and, I need the information yesterday."

It's a corny joke that when I first used, Heather had taken seriously and pouted for two days. Now, of course, she just sticks her tongue out at me.

In my office, a closet compared to the front area where Heather is ensconced, I turned my computer on. As the screen flickered with the pretty whirling colors, blinked off a few times, and did some more light work, I gazed out the window toward the Washington Channel. The high-rise condos that dwarf our little two-story building that looks like a country motel, only leave a little blue sliver of the channel and a slightly larger sliver of the Potomac River visible, and that mainly in the winter when the trees between the buildings have shed their leaves. In late May, what I saw was mainly the lush green foliage, the tops of buildings across the river in Crystal City, and the sky, which was light blue with diaphanous wisps of clouds. The trees were too high and thickly leaved for me to even get a glimpse of the topmast of sailboats going up and down the river.

There wasn't much more to see inside my office either. Other than my desk, two chairs, a three drawer filing cabinet in which I kept working case files, and a small bookcase containing five books that I rarely read, I had one hunting picture; a copy of a watercolor that Heather had cut from a magazine; and my autographed photo of former Chairman of the Joint Chiefs of Staff, General Colin Powell. In the photo, he was shaking my hand. The picture had been taken a short time before I retired from the army; I was a lieutenant colonel assigned to the Pentagon, and had met Powell at a briefing he'd given to junior Pentagon staff. Other than my discharge certificate and the Silver Star I'd been awarded in the closing days of the war in Vietnam, it was the only reminder of my time in the army I'd hung on to.

By the time I'd realized that there was nothing, inside or outside the office, worth looking at, the computer had stopped its light show and settled on the main screen that Heather had set it for. She'd also set it up so that I could put the cursor on a little box across the top of the screen and pick what I wanted to do. I had two choices; email or games. I chose games.

When I'm working a case, in the early stages I tend to make notes. Sometimes those notes are written in my cramped handwriting in one of the reporter's notebooks I keep in the cabinet; no more than two or three cases in a notebook; at other times, I noodle in my head. I just sit somewhere quiet and let the facts of the case swirl and whirl around my mind until the right facts connect with each other. I didn't have enough in the case *de jour* to waste paper on, so I went the noodling route.

Now, some people have to sit absolutely still in order to concentrate. I'm not one of those people. If I'm doing something with my hands, my brain seems to work better. Sometimes, listening to soothing music on the radio helps the synapses fire better. I didn't have a radio in the office. It had to be hands. A small, very small, part of my brain was watching what my hands did as I tapped the keys to make moves on the tiny green and white chess board, with the greenish-black and greenish-white chess pieces that sat in the middle of my computer screen. Heather keeps bugging me to buy a color monitor to replace my old black and white – actually black, white and green – monitor, but

I don't use the darn thing enough to spend three or four hundred bucks just to be able to see a natural color chess board.

As usual, the computer was winning, but, when I'm noodling it doesn't bother me.

Not that my musings took all that long. I didn't have a hell of a lot.

One dead woman, Geraldine Wallace, age 90, and friends with my clients, William Powdery and crew. Cause of death, as stated by the attending physician, heart attack and stroke; talk about a double whammy; but, on that point, my clients disagree with the doctor. I couldn't be sure what crime had been committed; the clients were hinting at murder, but, I was thinking it was something more pedestrian like negligence (maybe deliberate, which would make it manslaughter at least, I think) leading to her death, followed by the looting of her estate.

My main suspect, so far, was the officious Dr. Morgan Winthrop. Why? Well, he certified the cause of death, and if it wasn't truly a heart attack; that meant he'd lied, and the question then was, why? What did he have to gain from her death? I needed means, motive, and opportunity. He had the means and the opportunity, but I couldn't for the life of me figure his motive. Maybe, I thought, Heather would unearth something in her information searches.

Way down on my list of suspects was the irascible Teresa Arden, general manager of Shady Grove. I couldn't see where she had means or opportunity, and like Winthrop, I couldn't discern a motive, but there was something unlikeable about the woman. In fact, that was the main thing with Winthrop; I just didn't care much for him.

I pretty much dismissed the little redhead nurse, Wilomena Dunn. She seemed like such a cowed and mousy sort, I couldn't see her harming anyone. I'd still have Heather check her out, but I didn't see it going anywhere.

The rest of the staff at the center I discounted. I'd have them checked, but I couldn't see any of them having means or opportunity.

Then, as an afterthought, I decided to get Heather to run background checks on William Powdery, Helen Anthony, and George Madison. Sure, they were my clients, but that didn't mean they were clean. Maybe they did something to the old lady that the doctor missed, and hired me to divert suspicion.

You see; that's how my mental process of case review works. Most cases, I have more information, and there's a bit more meat. In this case, I barely had bones to hang any skin on. If Heather didn't come up with something, I wasn't sure what to do. I usually harass Buster Mayweather, but this wasn't a DC case, and I had no contacts in the Montgomery County Sheriff's Office. I thought about calling Quincy Chang, but then, I wasn't even sure what legal questions to ask him.

Dead end, dead end; sound of muffled drums in the background as the clueless private investigator goes down in flames to the chess playing computer yet again.

Chapter 9

I'd taken a hosing for four games when Heather poked her head around the edge of my door and jerked me out of my masochistic musings.

"Boss, I got a tidbit on that Dr. Winthrop that you might want to follow up on," she said.

Happily, I moved the cursor over the 'shut down' button, and glanced at the screen as it darkened.

"Okay, honeybunch," I said, using my pet name for her. "Whatcha got?"

"I called this friend of mine who works for the local medical association, and she just happened to know Winthrop. She gave me the name of a doctor here in the District who did his residency with him. She seemed to think you would find talking to him interesting."

Heather has a 'friend' in just about every office and organization in the Washington area, and they never seem to be shy about sharing corridor gossip with her.

"Probably wouldn't hurt. He might be able to give me a better sense of what kind of person Winthrop is. What's his name, and where can I find him?"

She came in and handed me one of those little yellow sticky sheets. She'd written on it in that precise script of hers. "Dr. Allen Fontaine," and an address that wasn't that far away; on Martin Luther King Jr. Avenue, across the Anacostia River opposite the Washington Navy Yard. I tucked the paper in my shirt pocket and headed out.

I debated taking the Metro, and then decided against it, since it would probably be close to lunch time by the time I finished talking to Dr. Fontaine. I drove up Fourth Street and then east on M Street to South Capitol. I turned right on South Capitol Street and drove across the bridge into Anacostia, an area of rundown buildings mixed in with the Naval Station, other government warehouses, factories, vacant lots, and a few historic buildings from the nineteenth century, including the house that belonged to Frederick Douglas. I turned northeast on Martin Luther King Jr. Boulevard and got into the far right lane, looking for the address.

Dr. Allen Fontaine's office was a two-story red brick building that was built in the early 1920s, with a gabled porch that wrapped around one side, and a paved parking lot off to the other side. There were weed-choked vacant lots on either side. The parking lot was empty except for a late model black and gray Volvo parked near the building.

I pulled in next to the Volvo.

The building had once been a residence, and the entrance parlor had been converted into a reception area, which was occupied by a cute brown-skinned girl who asked me to wait on one of the wooden chairs until Fontaine finished with a patient. There was one other patient, an elderly man with a bandage on the side of his neck, who sat leafing through a wrinkled magazine.

Fontaine, a short, rotund man with brown hair combed into a widow's peak atop his round head, cherubic cheeks, and twinkling blue eyes, came through an arched doorway behind a young black woman and a little boy. Spotting me, he nodded and smiled, and then turned back to the woman and said something I couldn't hear. The woman smiled and patted his arm. As she and the boy left, Fontaine came over to me. He extended a pudgy hand. His grasp was firm enough, but his palms were moist, and his skin was soft.

"You must be Mr. Pennyback," he said. He looked to be in his mid-forties, but he sounded like a pimply-faced teenager. "Your assistant called and said you were coming. Want to come back to my office?"

I followed him through the arched doorway, through a room that was probably once a living room, but that was now filled with diagnostic gear. Off to the sides were doors to other rooms; the doors bore signs identifying what lay behind them, including two marked only with pictures of outline characters representing a man and a woman. He led me to a door in the back.

His office was Spartan. A desk, one of the gray metal office kinds that you see at the DMV or the manager's office at your local garage, a swivel chair behind it, and another chair; one that didn't swivel; to the side, two three-shelf cases filled with medical books, and his med school degree on the wall. On one of the shelves was a picture of him with a slender blonde and two little boys.

He sat behind the desk and waited until I was seated in the free chair.

"Your associate, Ms. Bunche, said you wanted to talk to me about Morgan Winthrop." His round cherubic face wrinkled in a frown. "Mind telling me what this is about?"

"I'm working for a client who has an interest in Winthrop," I said. "So, I'm doing a background check; you know, talking to people who knew him, credit reports, stuff like that."

It wasn't totally untrue, and it was all he needed to know. He seemed satisfied. He nodded. I took out my notebook; it would look more credible if I took notes.

"Okay," I continued. "How long have you known him, and how well do you know him?"

"Well, I can't say I *know* him well; we were residents together nearly twenty years ago or more. I see him from time to time around town, or at some medical convention or other, but I wouldn't exactly call us friends."

I sensed a tension in his voice.

"You don't get along with him?" I probed.

"It's not like that. Like I said, we're not exactly friends; it's just that we rubbed up against each other during our residencies."

I leaned forward, my eyebrows raised. I don't like asking the obvious questions. He got the message.

"Well, see, our styles were so different," he said. "I was always taught to put the patient first; that's supposedly why we become doctors, to treat people. Morgan, on the other hand, is like a machine; cold and analytical. To him, a patient is just a vessel containing a medical puzzle for him to solve. I think he has more feeling for the diseases he treats than the people who suffer from them."

"I don't see how that would lead to conflict."

"I guess I was the cause of most of it. I couldn't help it; when I'd see the way he treated patients, I'd open my big mouth and criticize. Morgan doesn't take to well to criticism. He'd always call me a country sawbones who'd never rise above being an emergency room attending physician or a tiny practice in the sticks." He looked around, smiling. "Guess he wasn't too far off on that. He, on the other hand, saw himself heading a research department for some big company, or dean of some medical school."

"And yet, he's the head physician at an old folks' home."

Fontaine chuckled. "Yeah, I've never figured that one out. They must really pay well. That's Morgan's other fault that always got under my skin; he's fixated on being rich. Likes to show off his wealth."

"Do you think he's capable of doing something illegal?"

"You mean like prescribing drugs for addicts or something like that?"

"Well, yeah, something like that."

He looked at me, long and hard. His brow

wrinkled in concentration, like a man wrestling with himself.

"No, I don't think Morgan would go so far as to something so blatantly illegal." He had a sad look on his face. "I mean, it takes a person who cares about others as human beings to even do that, and frankly, when it comes to the practice of medicine, Morgan has a machine for a heart."

"You think he might deliberately make a mistake in treating someone?"

His brows, thin tendrils of hair that stuck out in all directions, lifted. "Why would you ask that?"

"Sorry, but I'm not at liberty to say. You didn't answer my question."

"Well . . . no, I don't think he'd deliberately misdiagnose a condition; he's too egoistic and self-centered for that. Look, has a patient of his died under . . . mysterious circumstances?

"Define mysterious."

He laughed; a mirthless barking sound. "You're a real cagy one, Mr. Pennyback. You're sitting on what I suspect is interesting information, but you won't tell me what it is; yet, you expect me to spill my guts to you."

"That's what private investigators do; ask questions in order to get answers. Do you tell your patients everything when you examine them?"

"Actually, I try and do just that," he said. "I think the patient has every right to know what we see and what we do, or plan to do. Now, Morgan is just the opposite. He believes that the average person lacks the intelligence to understand the details of a medical condition, so he's likely to tell them as little as possible. But, to your question, mysterious circumstance would be a person being seriously ill, or dying, and there was a question as to the true nature of the malady."

"Like, say, someone dies and a doctor says it was a heart attack, but other people thought it was something else?"

"Precisely; look, medicine . . . is still more art than science. Most doctors probably wouldn't want you to know it, but when they're diagnosing what's wrong with you, they're often guessing. Intelligent and informed guesses, but guesses nonetheless."

"You're not making me feel too good about having to go to the doctor."

"I'm not trying to scare you, but I find that an informed patient is more capable of participating in care that works. Like I said, doctors make intelligent guesses, backed up by years of training and experience. That said, it's still possible to make mistakes. Heart attacks, for instance, are a major cause of sudden death, yet, other conditions have symptoms similar to heart attack; severe heartburn or acid reflux for instance. While heart attacks are usually the result of long term underlying coronary problems, there are also certain toxins that can cause heart-attack-like symptoms, some medicines can react with each other to cause heart attacks, and there are even some foods that have chemicals in them that can react with medicine to cause heart attacks."

"Damn; how's a doctor to know what to do?"

"The careful physician, when a patient comes in exhibiting certain symptoms, does a thorough examination, starting with the most serious potential cause and working down. If you're going to administer the correct treatment, you have to know what the disease is."

"So, if a patient came in complaining of chest pains, dizziness, and pain in the arms, you'd check first for a heart condition?"

"Yes; that, and check the patient's history to see if there'd been previous complaints, or a family history of heart problems."

"What if you'd not seen the patient before?"

He leaned forward, looking at me strangely. "You haven't told me what this is all about, but I'm not stupid. I figure there was a death at the retirement center where Morgan works, and the family is considering malpractice charges. If that's the case, it's unlikely he wouldn't know the patient's condition and history; one of the things they do when old people check into places like that is insist on a medical exam. It protects them from liability, and assists the facility in providing proper care. Additionally, they'd probably require periodic examinations. The problem with Morgan is that he probably made an initial diagnosis based on the most common interpretation of the symptoms, but it turned out to be something else that didn't respond to treatment. When he and I were residents together, that was another thing we fought about; he'd never change a diagnosis once he made it."

He raised his eyebrows as if to ask, 'did I get that right?', but, I wasn't ready to tell him too much. I had a lot of questions I needed answering, and the people at Shady Grove would have to answer them. I didn't like stringing Fontaine along; he seemed a real straight-up kinda guy, and unlike most doctors, talked to me as if I was an adult instead of a child, but still recognized that I didn't understand the complicated medical terms that roll so easily off doctors' tongues. I respected that, and I suspect that all of his other patients did as well. I'd probably be coming back to him with more questions when I knew enough to ask them, so I wanted us to part on good terms.

"I can't tell you any more right now," I said.

"I have a bit more digging to do first. But, I promise I'll fill you in as soon as I can."

That seemed to please him. He smiled a knowing smile and nodded his head.

I didn't think the people at Shady Grove would be smiling when I next spoke with them.

Chapter 10

On the way back to the office, I saw a sign advertising 'authentic Mexican food,' on a squat brick building nestled between two warehouses, so I found a parking meter with a few minutes on it and parked. The place smelled authentic enough; the odor of refried beans and corn flour tortillas heavy in the air; and almost all the patrons were short, swarthy Hispanic looking types wearing workers' coveralls. I ordered a tamale, rice, and refried beans, which were quickly brought to my table along with a bottle of Corona beer. The food tasted authentic, and the beer was cold, and it was cheap by Washington standards.

I was still burping the tamale sauce taste when I got back to the office. Heather wrinkled her nose, but tactfully made no comment, as I sat near her desk.

"Did you get anything useful this morning?"

I asked.

She pulled a note pad from her drawer and flipped it open, rifling the pages until she'd found what she was looking for.

"There've been ten deaths at the center over the past three years. Now, just over three deaths per year isn't out of line for a home for the elderly; after all, old people die all the time. The two years before that there was one death each year. I've not been able to find anything more five years in the past. Of course, before 1996, many places like this didn't have computerized records, and a lot of the old paper records haven't been digitized yet."

I love Heather dearly, but like a lot of computer experts, she thinks everyone's as interested in the history and background of the infernal machines as she is. When she does what she calls a 'data dump,' it's often like being under the hind of an elephant that's just been given an enema.

"So, you found out that old people in homes for old people die; what does that have to do with our case?"

"Well, I looked into the causes of death where I could find them, and the histories of the people who died, and, you'll never guess what I found."

"Only if you force me to."

"Oh, you're no fun." I made a growling noise and frowned at her. "Okay, if you're going to be like that. What I found was, except for the two who died four and five years ago, all those who died within the past three years died of heart failure, and even more important, each one of them just happened to have no next of kin and a will leaving everything to Shady Grove."

"Was there a record of autopsies on any of them?"

"That was the third thing they all had in common; they all had death certificates signed by Dr. Morgan Winthrop, and no autopsies were required; oh, and they were all cremated."

"Didn't that raise warning flags for someone?"

"I thought so at first, but I checked the regulations. When a person dies in a nursing home, and the attending physician certifies the death and signs the death certificate, there's only an autopsy if someone can show suspicious circumstances. I couldn't find one case that required an autopsy. Afterwards, the body is released to the family for disposition. If they want to cremate, they only have to wait 48 hours, and if the local authority doesn't come forward to demand an autopsy, the deal's done, and that's the end of it. In most cases where there's no next of kin, the nursing home is responsible for disposition, and, they can pretty much do whatever they want. In all of the cases I found, everything was done by the book."

"Damn it; that doesn't leave us much to work with."

She got a hurt look on her face.

"Sorry, Heather; I'm not blaming you. It's just that I was beginning to believe those old people, and I was hoping you'd find some kind of smoking gun, or at least one with a warm barrel."

"Yeah, boss, I know; so did I. There is one thing that might be interesting. I checked the time between filing the death certificate and the cremation, and in each case it was done almost exactly 48 hours after the paper was turned in. I've never been there, but I can't believe they're that efficient."

"They're not really." I told her about what seemed to be a discrepancy in the victim's medical records.

"Are you going to check it out?"

"Damn straight I am. Did you get the contract drawn up?" She nodded, and pulled a two page document from her desk. It was a boilerplate contract we'd come up with that only required her to fill in the name or names of the clients and any special information. "Good; you can come with me and we'll go out and get it signed. You can get the signature and deposit while I do some snooping around."

"Okay," she said, smiling broadly. "One other thing before I forget; just on a hunch, I ran a check on this guy Burton Linde, the manager's boyfriend. He's not an American citizen; he's Canadian. Been staying here on some kind of work visa; he's some kind of musician."

"Are you sure of that? When I met him, I got the feeling he was a construction worker, and I'd never have pegged him for a Canadian from his accent. Interesting."

Chapter 11

We locked the office and drove both our cars to the center in Rockville. One of the advantages of being a two-man office, with me as boss; our hours can be as flexible as we want. I figured Heather could go on home as soon as she got the contract signed, and after I'd snooped around a little, I'd go on home and get supper started early. The tamales from lunch were already wearing off.

There were a few more cars in the lot than I'd seen on my first visit. We found spaces at the end of the visitor's lot; giving us a bit of a hike to get to the main building.

A young Asian man dressed in the blue of the male orderlies volunteered to escort Heather to William Powderly. I noticed that as he talked to her, his eyes never met hers; they stayed glued on a spot about six inches below her chin – actually, two spots – but, she didn't seem to mind, so I said nothing.

I told the receptionist that I wanted to speak with Winthrop.

The receptionist, a bright-faced young woman with spiked brown hair and too much eye makeup, spoke into the phone, hung up and looked up at me, smiling broadly. "Sorry, but Dr. Winthrop is in with a patient right now. Would you like to speak with Nurse Dunn?"

I'd *rather* speak to the doctor, I thought, but would *take* what was available, so I nodded. She asked me if I knew where Dunn's office was, and I said yes.

The little redheaded nurse was standing in front of the filing cabinet behind her desk, thumbing through folders in the top drawer. She jumped and spun around when I walked in, her eyes wide with fright.

"Oh, you startled me," she said. "Mr. Pennyback; what can I do for you?"

"I have a few more questions about the Wallace case, if you don't mind."

"I've already told you all I know about it. What more could you want to know?"

I sat down next to her desk, looking up at her. Her eyes blinked nervously as she fiddled with the folder she was holding. She took a deep breath and sat down behind her desk. "Okay, what do you want?" she asked. Her fingers were laced together, wiggling continuously.

I let her squirm for a few seconds, looking at her with a level gaze. There were little beads of sweat above her upper lip.

"I want you to walk me through what happened the day Geraldine Wallace died. Don't leave anything out, no matter how trivial it might seem."

"You should really talk to the doctor about that."

"I will, believe me, I will," I said. "But, I'd like your version of what happened."

She closed her eyes, and placed her hands over them pressing her brow into her palms. Without opening her eyes or looking up, she began speaking.

"Madeline, Ms. Wallace, came in around seven; maybe a few minutes before. I was here alone. Dr. Winthrop and I rotate evening duty to make sure there's someone around for just such situations." Her eyes opened now, but, she seemed to be looking at a point somewhere far behind me. "When she came in, she said she was feeling a pain in her chest and some discomfort, and wanted something for heartburn. I knew about her eating habits, so at first I didn't think too much of it, but after giving her an antacid, I decided to check her vitals; just to be safe you understand."

"Wouldn't you do that anyway?"

"In a normal clinic, yes; but, the residents here, some of them, can be real fussy. Unless there's a clear medical problem, the management insists we treat them with kid gloves. Some of them hate being poked and prodded. When I asked her if I could check her blood pressure and pulse, at first she refused. I don't remember what excuse I used, but I finally got her to go along. The readings worried me. Her pulse was irregular, and she had a blood pressure reading of 161 over 101; that's pretty high even in a younger person, but frightening in someone her age. Anyway, I asked her a few questions and discovered that she'd been having chest pains, difficulty breathing, and occasional nausea. I had her lie down on the table and immediately called the doctor."

"What happened after the doctor came?"

"He rechecked her vitals. I'd done it just before he came in but . . . well; Dr. Winthrop doesn't really trust anyone but himself. As soon as he saw her bp reading and the erratic pulse, he had me start prepping her for an ECG."

"So, he thought she might be having a heart attack?"

"I don't know what he thought at that moment; I certainly thought it was her heart. Of course, it wouldn't really matter; with those symptoms even a first year med student would assume a possible heart problem."

She was still playing with her fingers, and there was a little tic in her cheek, just below her right eye. I sat quietly, looking at her with a level gaze to let her know I wanted her to continue. She took a deep breath.

"I'd just about got all the leads connected," she continued. "When she sort of went into shock; she was trembling and her skin got all clammy. I've been a nurse for a long time, and I've seen a lot, but it started so quickly it freaked me. Well, there was no question of trying to do an ECG. Dr. Winthrop grabbed the defibrillator and tried shocking her, but she just stiffened and died. It was over so fast. He tried to bring her back; we alternated defib, chest pressure, and mouth to mouth; but, it was too late."

"So, he just declared her dead, called it a heart attack and that was that?"

"Well, yes; what else could it have been?"

Chapter 12

What else indeed?

I'd have given anything for the answer to that question. Well, almost anything.

I didn't think there was much more I'd get from Wilomena Dunn, so I planted myself outside the examination room of the clinic to grab Winthrop as soon as he came out, and before he could find another excuse to avoid me.

I hadn't been waiting long when a stoop shouldered old man with a cantaloupe pot belly and sparse strands of silver hair on his liver-spotted pate walked out, buttoning his shirt. Winthrop came out behind him. He didn't look happy to see me.

"Is there something I can do for you?" His voice was as cold as his expression.

"Yeah, I have a few more questions about

the Wallace case."

I can play the cold card too.

He looked around as if he was seeking an excuse to turn me down, but there were no other patients in the vicinity, and the old man had already disappeared from view.

"Very well; come to my office. But, I don't have a lot of time for you."

"It shouldn't take that long. I just need a few details that you didn't give me when we talked before."

"I told you everything that happened. There's really nothing else to add."

He was walking as he talked. When we arrived at his office, he went in, leaving the door open for me. He went behind his desk and sat; his eyes boring into me as I took the chair in front of his desk.

"Yeah, you told me a lot, but most of it was in medical jargon, and you were a bit skimpy on the details."

"Well, it's hardly my fault that you don't understand medicine well enough to follow what I said. I'm not accustomed to discussing my cases with laymen."

"Don't you have to explain things to your patients?"

"I'm not in the habit of going into great detail with them. I tell them what they need to know."

"And, it's you who decides what they *need* to know."

His eyebrows shot up and his lips turned down. He hadn't missed the sarcasm implicit in my statement.

"As a matter of fact, that's correct. The average person doesn't possess the knowledge to comprehend too much technical information. My patients can rest assured that I have their best interests at heart. My diagnoses and recommendations for their treatment and care are based on sound science."

"Someone just told me recently that medicine is more art than science; that you guys are guessing most of the time."

His face darkened, and his eyebrows did another little dance. "Whoever said that doesn't understand the medical profession."

"It was a doctor."

He blew noisily through his nose. "Not a very competent doctor I would imagine."

I smiled; more of a leer in fact; as I leaned forward, putting my hand on his desk. "Sort of like a doctor who might diagnose a patient with one illness; say, a heart attack; when, in fact, the patient has another problem?"

He opened his mouth to speak, and then snapped it shut. His eyes blinked rapidly for a few seconds.

"Are you trying to imply that I didn't handle the Wallace case correctly?"

"I'm not implying anything, doctor. I'm just asking questions. For instance, in this case, did you even consider that there might have been something other than your garden variety heart attack going on?"

"The patient presented clear symptoms of myocardial infarction. The likelihood of there being some other cause was far too remote to even consider."

"Had Geraldine Wallace ever had heart problems before?"

His eyes stopped blinking.

"Uh . . . well . . . I don't know."

"Aren't regular medical checkups part of the package people here pay for?"

"Yes, they are; but, routine physicals are conducted by my nurse. I only get involved if something turns up that indicates an illness or a potential problem."

"And, you were never told that Wallace had a history of heart problems?"

"No; and, if I had been told I would have

remembered."

There was something about him; his tone of voice or his attitude of disdain and superiority, or both; that bugged hell out of me. Trying to be nice to him in the hopes he'd be more cooperative wasn't working; probably never had a chance in hell of working in the first place.

"Did you even think of the possibility of something else being wrong with her?"

"No. It was a heart attack, pure and simple; complicated by a simultaneous stroke. There was nothing anyone could have done to save her."

"If you called it wrong, and didn't do the right thing, that's probably true," I said. "And, of course, you get to bury your mistake – or, in this case, burn it."

"How dare you . . . I don't make mistakes, and I resent your implication. I think this conversation is at an end, and if you have any plans to repeat any of this outside this office, let me warn you; you'll hear from our lawyers."

Chapter 13

I left Winthrop sitting behind his desk, red-faced and with his hand resting on the phone.

Teresa Arden caught up with me just as I was nearing the reception desk.

"Mr. Pennyback," she said in a cold voice. "Could you come with me to my office? We have to talk?"

I couldn't think of anything I wanted to talk to her about, but I didn't want to make a scene. I followed her back to her office.

"What do we have to talk about?" I asked as she dropped into her chair.

"You really put a burr up Morgan Winthrop's ass, you know. He nearly blew my ear off after you left. You didn't really accuse him of malpractice, did you?"

"Not directly. I did ask him if he was sure

he'd diagnosed Geraldine Wallace correctly. He didn't seem to like me even suggesting he might have made a mistake."

She laughed and slapped her hand against the desk. "Well, that explains his snit. Even hinting that the great god of medicine might have made a mistake is the same to him as accusing him of malpractice. According to him, he doesn't make mistakes. You're lucky he didn't throw something at you."

Now, it was my turn to laugh. "No, actually; he's lucky he didn't throw anything at me, because I would have caught it and thrown it back, and I don't think I would have missed."

She cocked her head to one side, smiling up at me.

"I do believe you would. Look, I understand what you're doing, and I'll try to sit on Winthrop. We don't need to get caught up in a public circus here. Just please, try not to provoke him any more than you absolutely have to, okay?"

"Okay, but if he did screw up in his diagnosis, then he should pay."

"Sure, I know; but, it's his word against yours if he sues you for defamation."

"In a court who do you think a jury will listen to; a smug asshole like him, or an average Joe like me just trying to get answers for a bunch of old people? Based on his reaction when I asked him about it, he'd look like shit on the stand. Hell, just being in court is enough to smear crap all over his reputation, so the smartest thing you can do is convince him to drop that idea."

She nibbled at her index finger. The look in her eyes was hard to fathom. It was as if she was looking at something behind me rather than at me.

"My, my; you do play hard ball, don't you?"

Chapter 14

As I walked out the front door of the Shady Grove administrative building, Heather came around the corner of the building with Powderly, Anthony and Madison in tow.

"Boss," she called. "Bill and his friends would like to talk to you."

I agreed, and they led us back to the little glen where I'd first met them.

We settled ourselves, the three of them together on a bench facing me. Heather sat next to me.

"Have you found anything?" Powderly asked. "Were we right? Geraldine didn't just have a heart attack, did she?"

They all leaned forward with expectant looks on their faces. I composed myself; preparing to deliver what I knew wouldn't be good news.

"I'm afraid not; at least, not yet."

Their faces wrinkled in consternation.

"But, Geraldine was as healthy as a horse," Helen Anthony said. "I just can't believe she'd have a heart attack like that. You must be missing something."

"I spoke to another doctor about the case," I said. "A heart condition could have gone unnoticed, and then just suddenly popped up. Do any of you know if she was taking any medication?"

Three heads shook in unison.

"She didn't even take aspirin," Madison said. "Said it upset her stomach the few times she did. That woman had the constitution of a horse; a race horse."

"Until the day she died, she hadn't even complained about a headache or anything," Powderly added. "Hell, that evening she ate a big meal. We usually order food from one of the local pizza places, but we decided to eat in the dining room. She put away as much as I did, and that's no mean feat; I'm a pretty good eater myself."

"Could something she ate have caused problems?"

"I don't see how; we all had the same thing, and none of us had any problems."

"Well, we didn't all have the same thing," Anthony said. "Remember, Geraldine had that piece of chocolate cake Ms. Arden gave her."

"Oh, yeah," Powderly said. "But, she didn't eat all of it. Said it wasn't sweet enough. She only ate about half of it."

"That's right," Madison said. "She didn't hardly eat enough of it to matter. That was nice of Teresa to do it. She doesn't usually join the residents in the dining room. Said she was so happy to see us there, she just had to come in and join the party. She had this big old chocolate cake she said a friend had given her and she couldn't eat it all."

"Did anyone else eat any of it?"

"I don't know. She came over to our table and offered to share it with us. I don't eat sweets, and old Bill here's lactose intolerant and can't eat stuff with milk in it."

"That's for sure," Anthony said. "You don't want to be around him if he eats cake or anything with milk." She wrinkled her nose.

"I can't help it," Powderly said. "Been that way all my life."

"Why didn't you eat any?" I asked Anthony.

"Can't stand chocolate," she said.

"So, your friend was the only one who ate

something different from anyone else? I don't know if that's important. I'll have to consult my doctor friend; but, I don't see how a small piece of cake could have caused a heart attack."

"What if it wasn't something she ate?" Powderly said. "Maybe they did something to her when she went to the clinic."

"I'm looking into that, but, it's not easy. The doctor and nurse are the only ones left who know what happened that night, and I don't expect either of them will confess to wrongdoing."

"You're not planning to give up on this, are you?"

"No, Mr. Powderly, I'll keep digging. If there's anything to be found, I promise you, I won't stop until I find it."

Chapter 15

The distance between making a promise and keeping it can sometimes be far. I meant it when I told Powderly and his friends that I wouldn't quite until I'd solved the mystery of Geraldine Wallace's death; but, I was at a loss as to just how I was going to go about doing it.

The next day, I called Allen Fontaine, but his receptionist informed me that his father had fallen ill and he'd had to go to Maine to visit him and wouldn't be back for a week. That left me with little to do but cool my heels.

The month of June sneaked up on me, and I'd made no progress. I went into the weekend in something of a blue funk because of it. Sandra, seeing the mood I was in, suggested we spend the weekend in Atlantic City, so we drove up and booked into the honeymoon suite at the big casino; making full use of the amenities usually reserved for newlyweds, and giggling at the way the hotel staff treated what they thought was an older couple on their second honeymoon. I dropped ten dollars in the slots, while Sandra inserted a quarter in a machine and hit the small jackpot.

I was feeling better by the time we got back to the farmhouse Sunday night, and woke up the next morning ready to tackle the bear in his den; if only I could find the damn thing.

Allen Fontaine had also returned to DC on Sunday. When I called him, he told me to come straight to his clinic.

Fontaine was waiting for me, and as soon as I entered the clinic, he motioned me to his office, telling the receptionist to hold everything but emergencies until we were finished.

"My girl said you sounded anxious over the phone," he said after we were seated in his little office. "Did you find out something since we met last?"

I went over what I'd learned from my visit to Shady Grove. He nodded, and made notes on a pad as I spoke. "So you see, doc, I don't know what I've learned."

"You just might have picked up a critical piece of information," he said. "You know, some foods can react with certain medications, causing such high blood pressure it can lead to fatal heart attacks. Do you know if the patient was on any kind of anti-depressant?"

"Her friends said she didn't even take aspirin. I got the sense she was a feisty old bird. They insist she was in prime health."

"Usually heart attacks are preceded by a period of coronary problems," he said, looking at his notes. "As people get older their arteries can become constricted, slowing the flow of blood to the heart and other organs. If the heart is deprived of oxygen-carrying blood, the result can be a heart attack. But, if the person was otherwise healthy, a sudden heart attack is unusual. One caused by medicines reacting with each other, on the other hand, is possible. You say this person ate chocolate?"

"Half a slice of chocolate cake, according to her friends; what could react with chocolate cake to cause a heart attack?"

"Some anti-depressants, like phenelyzine, can react with the tyramine in things like chocolate, bananas, sour meats, beer, cheese, and some other foods, causing extremely high blood pressure, which can be fatal."

"I have no idea what either of those chemicals is, but if I hear you right, she could have eaten something, and then been given medication, or taken medicine that killed her?"

He shook his head. "Unless she was senile, it's unlikely she would have taken it. Anyone on medication for depression would have been warned of the potential dangers. If the medical staff at the center prescribed the medication, or were aware of it, I should think they would also have warned her to avoid eating certain foods."

"Okay, I think I understand that. Is there anything else that can cause a heart attack?"

"I don't want to scare you," he said, laughing. "But, there are a number of things that can cause heart failure in otherwise healthy people. Too much exercise, excessive dehydration, or a combination of the two; taking in more fluid than the body can handle; a sudden fright. Hell, just about anything that can cause a rise in blood pressure can send it high enough to be really harmful."

I finally decided he might as well be fully informed. I gave him the details, including the patient's name. "Winthrop said she had a massive stroke as well."

"Well, I wasn't there, so I have to assume he read the signs correctly. A stroke at the same time as a heart attack; it would be hard to see the signs of a stroke if the heart attack killed her as quickly as you say he said it did. I don't imagine Morgan's in a mood to consider that he might have made a wrong diagnosis?"

I told him of Winthrop's threat to sue me.

"That sounds like him," Fontaine said. "He never did like to be contradicted; and, he could never admit a mistake."

"And, since he's burned this mistake, I guess there's no way to hold him accountable."

"I'm afraid you're right. Unless you can get him or his nurse to come clean on exactly what happened, there's nothing you can do legally. Unlike doctors working in a hospital, there's no real review of doctors who work in private clinics or nursing homes. If patients sue you for malpractice or file complaints, your cases might be looked at by the medical board, but otherwise, you're pretty much unsupervised."

I wanted to bitch about that not being right, but I realized that many doctors like Fontaine, who truly cared for their patients, took pains to do things right. I imagine he was a stricter critic of his performance than any board would be. Winthrop, on the other hand, struck me as incapable of doing anything but patting himself on the back.

I'd run into a brick wall that seemed too high to climb, that stretched too far to go around, and was set in granite, making it impossible to tunnel under. I'd have to find something to blow the sucker up.

I thanked Fontaine and rose to leave. He placed a hand on my arm.

"I'm sorry I couldn't be more help," he said. "There is one thing you could do, though; if you could get me a list of *any* medications she was taking, and everything, and I mean *everything* she ate or drank from about noon on the day she died, I might be able to do an alternate diagnosis."

"Thanks again. Can you do that without a body to poke and prod?"

"It's not perfect, and I wouldn't do it with one of my patients except in an extreme emergency; but, since the patient is already dead, you could call this a virtual post mortem."

Chapter 16

"Did you bother to ask him if he was married?" was Heather's comment after I told her what Allen Fontaine was doing for me. "He sounds like a real doll. Is he cute?"

Heather's only 32, but every day closer to 40, she acts as if her biological clock is about to run down; at least, that's the excuse she gives when I point out that she's been hitting on every man under fifty who has come near her.

"I think he's single, but maybe you should meet him before you start measuring him for a tuxedo." I told her about his request for a detailed list of Geraldine Wallace's last meal. "You can get with our clients and get the information; then, call Fontaine and arrange to deliver it. That way, you can make more progress on becoming a PI, and scope him out at the same time."

"Thanks, boss. I'll get right on it. In the

meantime, I got some more stuff on the folks out at Shady Grove. Dr. Winthrop worked at a hospital up in Baltimore right out of his residency, but only lasted two months before coming to Shady Grove. I don't know if his leaving a job so quickly was his choice or not; I'm still digging."

"Good job, honeybunch. You know, it's beginning to look more and more like this guy bungled and is covering it up. Let's see if we can nail his ass."

"One more thing; Teresa Arden, the manager; is up to her eyeballs in debt. Her house is in danger of foreclosure, and she has a ton of credit card bills. I don't know if that means anything, but wanted to flag it for you."

"Thanks. It probably means nothing; hell, everyone's in debt these days except you and me; but, I'll check it. See if you can find any connection between Arden and Winthrop other than working at Shady Grove."

Heather was reaching for the phone and I was just about to go into my office when Elizabeth Sung walked in.

In the presence of Carlton Raine, Elizabeth, though beautiful, stayed demurely in the background; walking into my office alone, she reminded me of how she'd been when I first met her. She had an aura of barely contained sexuality, like a smoldering ember, you could feel the heat simmering just below the surface.

She maintained her law practice in China Town, providing legal services to the old Chinese families who'd lived there for generations and who still didn't fully trust the *gwai lo*, or foreign devils outside China Town. She was wearing a yellow dress suit that accented her generous breasts, the curve of her hips, and the incredible length of her runway model's legs. Her face, translucent ivory with a flawless complexion, needed no makeup, and she wore little; a touch of eye shadow to accent her dark almond-shaped eyes and the barest hint of red on her full lips.

You might wonder why, being in a committed relationship with Sandra, I'd pay so much attention to Elizabeth? When we first met, she'd tried to seduce me. She'd been kidnapped and threatened with death by a Chinese mobster who was out to kill me, but, Buster Mayweather and I had rescued her with the help of a high-tech device from Carlton's collection of toys. When I introduced her to Carlton, it had been love at first sight – mixed with a generous helping of lust. So, it's safe for me to have lustful thoughts about her in my mind, because there's no danger of my ever acting on it, and I know she feels the same.

Confusing isn't it? That's the way life is sometimes.

"Elizabeth, what are you doing here?" I asked. Heather looked up and gave her one of those two finger waves.

"Carlton and I were discussing you this weekend," she said. "And, he thought it might be useful if I spoke to you."

I couldn't imagine what the two of them might have been discussing, but I was always happy to see her. After her attempt to seduce me at our first meeting, we'd become like brother and sister, and she and Sandra got along well.

"Sure; come on into my office."

I stood aside and let her enter. She took the chair in front of my desk, crossed her legs demurely, and waited for me to take my seat.

"Carlton was worried that you might have thought he was upset with you after you and Sandra visited," she said. "He wanted me to assure you that he wasn't."

In truth, I had detected a bit of tension between us after my rant against Cold War tactics, but I hadn't thought much about it.

"He needn't have worried. I probably owe *him* an apology; after all, I was going on about something that was important to him."

"It is, Al; but, not as important is your friendship. Besides, he knows you were right.

There has to be rules or we all descend to the level of beasts."

"I'm glad he didn't take what I said personally, but, I'm curious; why didn't he tell me this himself?"

"You know how he is; some things are hard to say to another man. He wants you to know that he loves you like a son, but he can't say it. I mean, he sort of says it to me."

I thought of him like a father, but, like him, I'd probably never be able to tell him that. I just grunted.

"I can see why you two are attracted to each other," she said. "You're exactly alike; a rigid sense of justice, and an inability to express emotion. Anyway, he also wanted me to share some more thoughts he had on the case you asked him about."

"Sure, I'm always interested in Blood's views."

She made a face; a wrinkling of her nose that caused her eyes to cross slightly. "I wish you wouldn't use that name. I hate it, because it makes me think of what he once did for a living. Anyway, I'm not sure I understand what he told me, but I'll try to pass it along like he told me . . . he said to look for who might profit from a situation, and to remember that it's not always about money. See who has ties to whom and how those ties might motivate them. Oh yes, and he said, it's not always about the victim. Does any of that make any sense to you?"

"As a matter of fact it does."

"Good, because I have no idea what it all means."

"I think I do, and if he's right, I'll come out and explain it to you – and thank Blo - , er, Carlton."

She smiled and stood. "Well, I probably have clients waiting, so I'll be on my way. Don't be too long coming to see us again, okay?"

I assured her I wouldn't, and thanked her for coming.

When she'd gone, the scent of her perfume still hanging in the air around my desk, I pulled out a note book and began making notes. I understood what Blood meant, and all I had to do was find the blocks and then the lines connecting them.

There are only a few reasons people kill other people, other than serial killers who do it for some inner compulsion or for kicks, or professional hit men who do it for the money; anger, greed, revenge, or money. Greed and money might seem related, but it could be greed for power or some other advantage. I didn't see anyone killing Geraldine Wallace for anger or revenge; and, that left greed and/or money.

I hadn't completely discounted that Winthrop had screwed up his diagnosis and was stubbornly refusing to own up, but, the money angle pushed Teresa Arden high up the suspect list. If she was having money problems, getting her hands on money and other convertible assets would be a priority. The problem was figuring out how she could have arranged the death. My guess was that it was most likely poison; which brought to mind the chocolate cake that no one remembered anyone but the victim eating. Of course, like the corpse, there was no evidence left that I could use to prove it. I'd have to get Heather to research the various poisons that might cause symptoms similar to heart attacks, and then I'd have to figure out how Arden might have done it.

Chapter 17

Buster called at half past eleven and invited me to join him for lunch at Mom's.

I of course agreed immediately. We hadn't eaten at Mom's in a long time, and I missed it.

Mom's is a soul food place on Sixteenth Street. A one-story stone building painted a sickly beige color with a large plate glass window in front and a hand-lettered sign that says, *Mom's*, and nothing else. If you don't know what they sell, you probably don't belong, or wouldn't like it. Mom's has been at the same location for longer than most people in the neighborhood can remember, with the same overweight brown-skinned woman wearing the same checkered apron running it too. Rumor has it that during the riots after Martin Luther King, Jr. was assassinated, Mom's was the only building on her street that escaped some kind of damage; in fact, some people say that the rioters took breaks from smashing store windows and grabbing TV sets to have lunch at Mom's. I've never been able to prove that story, but Mom is a force to be reckoned with. When you eat there, she tells you what's on the menu and what you're having; doesn't allow cursing, smoking, or spitting on the floor; and, you'd better clean your plate. Everything's fried except the biscuits and sweet potato pie. Cholesterol levels probably rise fifteen percent after a meal at Mom's, but it's the best tasting food in town.

Mom is a lot like her building; of indeterminate age, but enduring. She's about five feet tall and almost as wide across in the hips, with arms that are the same circumference from shoulder to wrist. She has a round face, dark brown and angelic looking, with large brown eyes that seem to be laughing even when she's pissed at you. She wears her hair plaited and wound around her head, usually covered by a light colored scarf tied in the front, making her look like that woman on the old pancake mix boxes, before political correctness forced the company to remove her. I don't know Mom's real name; you don't stick your nose into her business if you want to keep it intact; she's just Mom to everyone who knows her.

As usual, I found a place to park near the building; a lot of Mom's clientele comes from the laborers working in the vicinity, and most of them walk. Mom's imposing figure discourages people from parking in front of the building and then going elsewhere.

The smell of frying chicken, freshly baked biscuits, greens with fatback, and all the other greasy aromas that accompany the cooking of soul food, hung in the air like a comfortable blanket. Buster, all six feet of him, sat at our usual table in the right corner where he could keep an eye on the sidewalk outside and the entire interior at the same time. He'd saved the chair with its back to the wall for me. I hate sitting with my back to the door in a public place.

Mom was sitting on the stool behind the counter near the cash register. She smiled her gap-toothed smile at me as I entered.

"Well, if it ain't Mr. Pennyback. How you doin' hon; ain't seen you in a powerful long time."

"Doing fine, Mom; been busy. What's good today?"

"Same's always; everything's good. Jest you set yourself down and I'll get the cook to whup up somethin' good. You want coffee?"

I nodded. Mom's coffee is fresh brewed and has chicory in it; a custom she says she learned from her grandma.

Buster waved as I neared the table. He'd taken lately to shaving his head, but had grown a goatee, which, along with his Fu Manchu moustache, college running back shoulders, and narrow waist, made him look even more threatening than usual.

"Hey, bro," he said. "What's up? What kinda bad guys you chasin' nowadays?"

I plopped down next to him. Mom was right on my heels, placing a steaming cup of coffee at my elbow. She smiled and patted my shoulder. She always calls me 'mister,' but treats me like a favorite son. She calls Buster 'mister' too, but treats him more like a prodigal son because of his tendency to break her rule on cursing. She's always threatening to ban him from the place, but we all know she won't – or at least, Buster hopes so. His wife Alma won't serve fried foods, and it's the only place he can eat the food he likes.

I took a sip of coffee. It was strong, but the chicory cut some of the bite. "I've been busy for the past week," I said. I filled him in on the case. "So, you see, I'm sort of in a corner. I'm pretty sure somebody did something wrong, I just can 't figure out who or what they did."

"Shit; ain't much different than any of the other strange cases you got yourself mixed up in. You got no body; got no evidence; just one of them hunches of yours. What you gone do?"

"Just keep digging I guess. If I can find some kind of leverage, maybe I can get someone to spill. You order your food yet?"

"Naw; when I told Mom you'd be here, she said I had to wait. 'Sides, you know she always just gives us what she wants us to eat. Reckon it'll be good; always is."

I couldn't disagree with that. Mom's was like one of those Italian restaurants where the proprietor tells you, "Donta you worry, I'll takea care of everything. You gonna like it." And, you always did.

"You got any ideas? I know this case is out of your jurisdiction; but, maybe you could run some interference with the cops in Rockville."

"Just 'cause this place's in Rockville don't mean the city cops would have anything to do with it. It was probably the county cops got called, and if they thought there was a case, they'd turn it over to the state boys. But, you said the cop your man spoke to didn't even take a statement, so I doubt even the state cops would be interested."

I knew what he meant. Some bored county cop took Powderly's call, heard what the old man had to say, and dismissed it as the ravings of a semi-senile senior citizen with too much time on his hands. Probably wouldn't be anything but a brief notation in the files that he'd taken the call and found no evidence of a crime. End of the line.

"So, unless I can come up with something, this is worse than a cold case."

"Yeah," he said. "Ain't no case at all. I tell you what I can do, though; I can do some discrete checks on the folks who work there. Give me their names."

I took my notebook out, tore out a page, and wrote the names of the three main people at Shady Grove. I handed it across to him. After a brief glance, he put it in his pocket.

Mom brought our lunch; two plates heaped with golden brown fried chicken, thighs and breasts, a mound of mashed potatoes covered with brown gravy, collard greens with little chunks of fat meat, and huge chunks of cornbread. After she put the plates in front of us, she went back to the counter and drew two large glasses of iced tea and brought the frosted glasses back along with two slices of lemon.

We ate in silence, except for the scraping sound of knives and forks on the plates, and the occasional smacking sounds as Buster cleaned his plate in record time.

After finishing our food, we had more lemonade. Buster sat back in his chair, massaging his midsection, a satisfied look on his dark brown face.

"Now, that's what I call a meal," he said. He burped loudly, which drew a frown from Mom. "Sorry, but that just feels so good. Hey, bro; when you gone come visit. The twins growin' like weeds, and they been askin' when Uncle Al and Aunt Sandra gone come see 'em again?"

I sipped my lemonade, trying to duck answering him. His kids are cute, but, I'm even less comfortable around children than old people. I never know what to say to them until they can talk like grownups. I've never been one to engage in baby talk.

"Uh, soon as I finish this case, we'll have to get together."

He laughed and pulled at his goatee. "Yeah, you been sayin' that for weeks. Hell, if you'd go 'head and make an honest woman of Sandra and you two started makin' babies, you wouldn't be so skittish 'round kids."

Another subject I avoided. Sandra and I had a good relationship. I loved her, and had no doubt that she loved me in return, but neither of us was quite ready to take the next step. Even though she was a teacher, and really into her students, like me, she didn't seem to be anxious to have them around all day. Besides, at 40, she was a bit past safe childbearing age, and I was too old to think about being a father again.

"Hey, I promise; as soon as this case is finished, we'll do a weekend thing at your house. You can burn some more steaks on that grill of yours."

He grimaced. "Sorry, bro; it'll have to be

chicken or pork chops. Alma don't let me eat red meat no more. Says I got to watch my cholesterol or some shit like that. Way she's feedin' me at home, I'm gone be the healthiest corpse in the funeral home when I go."

"She's a smart woman, so you're better off listening to her. I gotta run now, but give me a call if you come up with anything, okay?"

I got up to leave. Mom came over. "Hey, hon, you leavin' 'fore dessert? I done made some key lime pie. Jest the thing after a meal of fried chicken."

"Thanks, Mom; maybe next time. I've got some urgent business to attend to."

"Well, I don't," Buster said. "Bring me a slice of that pie."

As I walked out, he was sitting there, a broad smile of anticipation on his face.

Chapter 18

Heather had her notebook open on her desk when I got back to the office.

"Ready for a data dump?" she asked. "I got a few more tidbits for you."

"At your desk or in my office?"

She looked up at me, and then down at the notebook, then she looked back up at me.

"Okay, at your desk."

I turned the chair around and straddled it, my arms resting on the back.

"Aren't you going to take notes?" she asked.

"Why should I? You have it all written down already."

I felt the blast from the frosty look she gave me.

"Okay, let's start with from the top. I've dug into Dr. Winthrop's background to a fare the well. Except for the fact that he's arrogant and has a shitty personality, there's nothing on his record that would indicate he'd ever intentionally harm a patient."

"Yeah, but was there anything that pointed to the possibility of him being wrong about what was ailing a patient?"

She flipped the page, and ran her finger down it. "A couple of the people I talked to did agree that that was possible. He doesn't like changing his mind on anything, because he can't believe that he'd be wrong, and, at the nursing home there's no one in authority to look over his shoulder. He's not having any financial problems; in fact, he comes from a fairly wealthy family."

"So, we can rule out homicide, but not malpractice, which is a form of negligent homicide."

"Yeah, but good luck proving it. You have no evidence."

"You don't have to keep reminding me of that," I said. "I'll just have to find it."

"You really have a case about this guy, don't you? Why are you so sure Ms. Wallace died because of something he did?"

"Oh, I don't know; maybe because he was

the attending physician who said it was a heart attack and wasn't able to save her? Maybe it's because he's such a dick, I just want him to be guilty."

"Boss, if everyone with a lousy personality was guilty of criminal behavior, we wouldn't have enough jails in this country to hold them. You know, there could be another answer."

"Being a shithead should be illegal. If there aren't enough jails, we could put them on some island in the middle of the Pacific and let them drive each other crazy. As for another answer, I'm open to suggestions."

"Well, Teresa Arden's having money problems. She'd certainly have motive to try and get her hands on the old lady's estate."

"I thought about that, but there's the problem of means and opportunity. She'd have to have access to the clinic and the knowledge to create a heart attack."

More flipping of pages and running her well-manicured fingers across rows of her neat script. "I don't know about opportunity, but I do know she has medical knowledge. Did you know that Ms. Arden, before getting her business degree and moving to management, went to nursing school?"

If I didn't before, I did now. That put a whole new light on things.

"Did you find out why she left nursing?"

"She didn't actually leave nursing. She dropped out just before graduating and re-enrolled in business school. I'm still trying to find out why she that."

"Probably thought there was more money in it; not that it seems to have done her much good."

"She gets a good salary, but for the past couple of years she's been living beyond her means. Her credit card bills alone look like the budget of a small country."

"Okay, I'll take a run at her. By the way, did you get that information Dr. Fontaine asked for?"

"Of course," she said. "I called Mr. Powderly first thing this morning and got a complete list of everything he remembers Geraldine eating, and I passed it to the good doctor."

"Good; what did he have to day about it?"

She closed her notepad and looked at me with a strange, half-smiling expression. "I'll let you know tomorrow," she said.

"Huh? Why can't you tell me now?"

"Allen said he'd tell me about it over dinner tonight."

Chapter 19

Heather was useless for the rest of the day; mercifully short. She sat behind her desk with a sort of vacant smile on her face, and humming to herself. I hadn't thought much about her personal life; obviously it had been a while for her. So, I cut her some slack.

For the first time since we started working together, she didn't hang back when I suggested we close up early. In fact, she had her purse under her arm and was heading for the door almost as soon as I'd said it.

That left me to lock up; not much of a problem since we have Yale locks on the filing cabinets, which only contain case files, and nothing we work on qualifies as national security. Our computers are a few generations out of date. No burglar worth his salt would bother stealing them; assuming there was a burglar desperate enough to even think about hitting our building. The area of the District where our office is located is under gentrification, with high rise condos and shiny office buildings going up all over, but our building is a holdover from a less prosperous past; a two story box-like structure that looks like one of those two-story motels for truckers you see along I-95 heading south.

The building is an old wooden structure with a slate roof, and it's badly in need of painting. I give the landlord credit; he at least keeps the parking lot and the tiny strips of grass and shrubbery around the place neat, and in all the time we've been occupants I've never seen a rat. Happy to have the place fully occupied, and taking no chances that any of us will get pissed and refuse our leases each year, he's only raised the rent four times in the past ten years.

So, locking up is not a big issue – it's just that I was so accustomed to Heather being there when I left, I hadn't done it in a while. It took me nearly an hour to make sure I'd locked all locks, emptied the waste baskets, turned off the computers, and set the answering machine in case someone called us after hours.

I was feeling smugly proud of myself during the drive across the District, along the Potomac on Whitehurst Freeway and then to Canal Road, up through Kensington and to River Road, my preferred commute. Not many bosses could take care of routine office chores – or so Heather was fond of telling me from time to time.

Sandra was home already, wearing tight jeans and a tee shirt, busy in the kitchen mixing salad. I eased up behind her and put my arms around her waist, pressing against her hips.

"You're getting sloppy in your old age," she said, pressing back against me. "I heard you come in."

"I wasn't trying to sneak up on you. Believe me, if that had my intent, you wouldn't have heard me."

She put the two large forks down on the counter and squirmed around until her breasts were spearing my chest – well, considering their softness, spearing is not the precisely correct word; more like caressing. "Okay, what's on your mind? And, why are you so late getting home?"

I filled her in on the lack of progress on the case, and on Heather's romantic conquest; it was difficult to maintain my train of thought because she kept gyrating her hips and pressing into me with a wicked smile on her otherwise angelic face.

I finally gave up. "You're not really interested in any of this, are you?"

She snaked her arms around my neck, pulling my head down until our lips met. The meeting of yielding flesh, followed quickly by the searching probing of her tongue drove thoughts of the case into the storage nook in the basement of my mind. Fortunately, she hadn't set the table for supper, so we didn't have broken and scattered plates and glasses to clean up afterwards.

We showered and dressed in matching jeans and Dallas Cowboy pullovers – Sandra wasn't a football fan, but she often wore Redskins paraphernalia because many of her students were diehard fans; after more than a year, I'd finally convinced her to be an equal opportunity fan – and, went back to the kitchen. The unfinished salad still sat on the counter. The lettuce was looking a little limp and wilted. I could sympathize.

We junked the salad and I heated a pan of leftover chili from the fridge. We had that with crackers and beer, and then, with bottles of Corona beer, settled on the sofa listening to classical music on the local National Public Radio station.

"You were saying something about Heather making out with one of the subjects in your current investigation?"

"He's not exactly a subject; more of an advisor. He's helping me make sense of the medical aspects. He invited Heather to dinner tonight." Frankly, while I liked Fontaine from the first meeting, I didn't think he had it in him. Just goes to show how judging from initial impressions can be wrong.

That thought made me wonder whether or not my first impressions in the case hadn't led me down a wrong path. I'd instantly disliked Morgan Winthrop because of his arrogance and aloofness. As a result, I'd been looking at him as the prime suspect; assuming that he'd screwed up and his ego was causing him to deny it. There was every reason to think that Teresa Arden could be the culprit. Her financial problems for one thing, and then, the fact that she had some knowledge of medicine made her as much a suspect as the doctor. I only had to prove it.

"I hope it turns out okay for Heather," Sandra said. "Allen sounds like a real nice man."

I shrugged and took a long pull from my beer. "Yeah, he seems to be a real standup kind of guy. Maybe she'll get lucky."

She put her bottle down on the coffee table and turned, taking my bottle from my hand. "Speaking of getting lucky, that chili is completely digested."

Chapter 20

When I got to the office the following morning, Heather was there, sitting behind her desk with a loopy smile on her face. I didn't need to ask why; it was obvious that she'd gotten 'lucky.' I probably had something of a loopy grin on my own face.

"Morning, honeybunch," I said. "What's the news?"

Her head turned and she looked up at me with a dreamy look in her eyes. "Huh?"

"Earth to Apollo, come in please," I said. "Did Fontaine tell you anything useful last night?"

"Yeah, he said I have beautiful eyes."

"I mean, about the case."

"Oh, yeah; he had a lot to say about that."

"And, you will share it with me, your

partner, sometime this century?"

She shook her head, causing her blonde hair to wave back and forth in front of her eyes. "Uh, yeah, sure; sorry, boss. Let me get my notebook." She fumbled around in her desk drawer, and then pulled the note pad out. "Here it is," she said, flipping pages. "According to Bill Powderly, Geraldine had sauerkraut and sausage in addition to that piece of cake. Oh, and she'd had a beer just before dinner. The rest of the things she ate don't matter."

"What the hell do sauerkraut, sausage, beer, and chocolate cake have in common?"

"According to Allen, they all contain something called tyramine, and if, after eating them she somehow got an antidepressant like phenelyzine into her system, it would have made her heart rate go up high enough to kill her."

"Did he say it was likely that Winthrop might have administered the drug?"

"No; in fact, he said it would be highly unlikely. Even if she was suffering from depression, he said, no doctor would give her anti-depression medication if she was showing signs of some kind of cardiac distress. Allen's convinced someone else would have to have done it."

"Someone with knowledge of medicine and

access to the victim; someone like Teresa Arden."

She closed her notebook and looked at me with a quizzical expression. "How would she get access? She's the manager of the place, but surely she wouldn't have free run of the clinic."

I wasn't so sure of that. Teresa Arden struck me as someone who pretty much got whatever she wanted and went wherever she chose to go. There was also the fact that her office was in the same corridor as the clinic, and she had come into the nurse's office without knocking. She could have walked into the clinic; the problem was, could she have done it without being seen by Winthrop or Dunn? I made a note to visit the clinic and take a look at the layout.

Then, a thought struck me. "She could have done it when she gave Wallace the cake in the dining room. You need to check with Fontaine and see if it's possible to administer a medicine like this any way other than injection."

She smiled broadly. "I'll ask him at lunch today."

"Dinner last night, and now lunch; you and the doctor seem to be hitting it off."

"You could say that." Her smile spoke volumes.

Chapter 21

I drove out to Shady Grove, taking cross town streets to the Fourteenth Street Bridge and then George Washington Parkway to I-495, the Beltway. I fought my way to the far left lane, dodging the idiots who weave back and forth from lane to lane in their efforts to get one more car behind them, keeping within the posted speed until I got to the I-270 split. On I-270, with the trucks competing with SUVs and vans for space, I worked over to the local lanes, which were only marginally less chaotic, until I got to exit 6B, which takes you to Route 28 west, going out toward the rural parts of Montgomery County.

Shady Grove's parking lot was again almost empty, and I parked as close to the administration building as possible, next to the black Mercedes which I assumed belonged to Winthrop, careful to leave enough space so my door wouldn't touch his when I got out. Bad enough that he might sue me for accusing him of incompetence; I didn't need a damage claim on top of it.

I guess I'd become something of a fixture; the receptionist, a middle-aged Asian woman, just looked up, and, when she saw me, waved me through.

Teresa Arden was sitting in her office, reading the *Washington Post* and sipping at a cup of coffee when I entered.

"Mr. Pennyback," she said, looking up. "What are you looking for this time? I should think you learned all you could during your last visit."

I straddled the chair next to her desk and propped my elbows on the back. "There's always something more to be learned. For instance, the fact that you're currently having some serious financial problems." Her eyes widened, and her cheeks colored. "I mean, money is one of the motivations for people to do harm to other people."

"I don't see how my financial situation has anything to do with one of our residents dying," she said. She'd closed the paper and folded it, the long-nailed index finger of her right hand tapping a photo of the DC mayor just below the masthead. Her left index finger was looped through the cup handle, but I could see that her hand was trembling.

"Well, the deceased did leave all her property to the center, did she not?"

"Of course, she did; as do many of our residents; but how does the center getting someone's estate affect my finances?"

"I'm assuming that as general manager, you have control of the center's budget and financial affairs."

"Uh, well, yes I do as a matter of fact, but for official center business. Are you suggesting that I might be using the center's money personally?"

I just looked blankly at her, raising my right eyebrow slightly.

"Whoa, buddy," she said. "I'll have you know I've never ever done anything like that. That would be fraud, and I've invested too much in my career to throw it away doing something stupid like that. Besides, even if I had done something like that; and, I'm saying I haven't; but, if I had, how would I have killed Geraldine Wallace? And, that's what you're really saying, no matter how you phrase it."

"Oh, the how part's easy." I spoke slowly; one, so I could remember everything Heather had told me, and two, so I wouldn't tell her too much. "It would just be a matter of somehow introducing something into her system to cause her to have a heart attack, or at least, symptoms that would look a lot like a heart attack."

She laughed. "And, I'm supposed to be smart enough to do that? Excuse me, but that would take someone with a lot of medical knowledge."

"Like someone who attended nursing school?"

The color left her cheeks. The drumming index finger froze in midair, poised over the mayor's face. The hand holding the coffee cup, though, shook enough to cause ripples in the liquid.

"You gonna deny that you went to nursing school; nearly graduated too, but dropped out at the last minute?"

She breathed out, a heavy, audible sigh, that seemed to deflate her. "Okay, so, yeah, I was in nursing school. I was a damn good student, too. But, I got tired of seeing sick and suffering every day; day in and day out, and, there was fuck all I could do about it other than empty their bedpans and wipe their asses when they messed on themselves. I decided there had to be a better way to make a living."

"But, you admit you have the knowledge to cause someone to have a heart attack; you could put something in them to do it?"

"Sure, I know the chemicals that could do

that. There's just one problem; how would I do it without Mr. Smartass Winthrop discovering it?"

I wouldn't admit it to her, but, that bothered me too. I still hadn't seen the layout of the clinic. But, she'd concealed information, and that's usually a sign of guilt over something. "From what I've seen of the good doctor, if it looked like a heart attack; and, he's made it quite clear that that's what he thinks it was; he'd look no further."

"He, you . . . he what? Winthrop might be a total ass, but he's a first rate doctor. I can't believe he'd be that stupid as to misdiagnose something like that, or to let something like that happen. I mean, you're right, someone with knowledge of medicine could do it, but they'd have to have access to the patient, and other than running into her and her friends in the dining room, I had no contact with Geraldine. You can check with her friends on that."

"You gave her a piece of chocolate cake in the dining room, right?"

"Well, yes I did. My boyfriend got it from someone at the club where he works and brought it to me. I was so happy to see that bunch deciding to socialize with the others; I thought I'd share it with them. I offered some to everyone to them, but she was the only one who accepted. And, she only ate half a slice. What does that have to do with anything?"

"Correct me if I'm wrong, but wouldn't the chemicals in the chocolate in that cake react with some medicines; say, medicines for treating depression; to cause a heart attack?"

Both her eyebrows arched and rose. A half smile creased her face. "I'm impressed. You've obviously done your homework. Yes, the tyramine in chocolate would combine with an anti-depressant to cause high blood pressure. But, it would take a large quantity of both to elevate blood pressure high enough to be immediately dangerous, and, like I said, she only ate a small amount of the cake."

"But, she also had sauerkraut and sausages, which also contain this tyramine stuff, doesn't it? Oh, and, I'm told she'd had a beer just before supper."

"Ah, well, yes, it she'd ingested all that, there'd be a pretty high concentration of tyramine in her system. But, that leaves the reacting chemical. As far as I know, she wasn't on any medications, for depression or anything else. And, in order to get enough in for it to be dangerous, it would almost have to have been injected. Tell me; how did I do that?"

"I was hoping you'd tell me."

She sat back in her chair, looking at me with wide eyes. Then, she laughed. "You're a real piece of work, Al Pennyback. You had me going for a minute there. You can't seriously think I killed Geraldine Wallace?"

"At this point, I don't know what to think," I said. "If you didn't do it, it means the doctor made a terrible mistake when he treated her."

She leaned forward, a broad smile on her face. "You mean, there's a possibility that Winthrop fucked up; that he misdiagnosed her and that led to her death?"

"I'm looking at that possibility."

"Finally, I have that bastard where I want him. Let's see him wriggle out of this one."

"Mind telling me what you're talking about?"

"It's nothing . . . not important," her eyes were flickering from side to side.

"You're lying, and that's not the way to convince me you've done nothing wrong."

"Oh hell, might as well tell you," she said. "I've been trying to get that jerk fired for the past year or more. I'm supposed to be the person in charge here, with him just responsible for health care; but, he acts as if he's the boss. If you must know, I can't stand him and his superior airs; so, if you prove he committed malpractice, his ass is history."

"Sorry to disappoint you, Ms. Arden," I said.

"But, if you repeat anything I've said to you here, I'll deny it, and that might not look too good for you if I find evidence that points in your direction."

"Huh! What would that be? Poor Geraldine's been cremated." She smiled. It was the smile of a cat about to pounce on a bird. "Doesn't matter. I can wait. When you do finger him, I won't have to do a thing. The board will can his ass."

"Long as you know I don't work for you."

"Sure, I understand. Look, you can ask the others here. I didn't go anywhere near that woman except in the dining room, and I didn't single her out. In fact, I offered the cake to Bill Powderly; she's the one who asked for a piece."

Chapter 22

"Well, yeah, as a matter of fact," William Powderly said. "Ms. Arden did offer me some of the cake; and, yeah, it was Geraldine who asked for a slice."

I'd found him in the little cottage he occupied, not far from the little glade where we'd met previously. He and George Madison were playing gin rummy at a card table in the tiny living room.

"Yeah, that Geraldine had herself an appetite," Madison said. "She could out eat the two of us."

They kept playing cards while they talked. Gone was the righteous anger I'd sensed in them when we first met. They now talked about Wallace as if she'd just popped out to the 7-11 for a pack of smokes. I guess death is taken that way when you get old; sort of like being a soldier in combat. When you know death is just around the corner and can strike at any moment, you tend to demystify it; it becomes almost a joke. Admittedly a macabre joke, but that's just one of the ways the mind copes with that over which you have no control.

"Let's focus, guys," I said. "I'm trying to find out what happened to your friend, so you gotta help me here. Do you think Teresa Arden would have any reason for wanting to hurt her?"

"Ms. Arden, oh no," Powderly said. "She can be a bit persnickety sometimes, but I don't think she'd hurt anybody."

"Oh, I don't know," Madison said. "I think she'd like to ram something up Dr. Winthrop's stuck up butt."

"She don't like him, that's for sure," Powderly said.

"Like oil and water, the two of them are," said Madison.

"Want to give me some specifics?" I chimed in to stop their Abbot and Costello routine.

They stopped their card game, hands holding fans of cards in midair, and looked at each other.

"Well," Powderly said. "There was the time Ms. Arden almost threw a book at the doctor."

"You mean that time when he called her a

penny-pinching witch?" Madison asked.

"Yeah, that's the time. He wanted to buy some newfangled machine for the clinic, and she told him they didn't have enough money."

"He didn't like being turned down, that's for sure."

"Not at all; but, that Ms. Arden, she's one tough broad."

I could see that this was their way of conveying information; I wasn't going to be able to get them to stop their two-man standup routine. Might as well play along; as long as it got me the information, I suppose it really didn't matter.

"Anything else?" I asked.

"Well," Powderly said. "There was the time the doctor was chewing that nice Ms. Dunn out in front of everybody."

"Ms. Arden lit into him something fierce," Madison said.

"Thought for sure she was gonna hit him."

"Or strangle him."

"Yeah, that's the first time I saw him looking scared. I think he thought that too."

"I hear Arden's trying to get the doctor fired," I said.

"Wouldn't surprise me," Powderly said.

"Nope, wouldn't surprise me either," Madison agreed.

I was beginning to get into the swing of their conversational style; just let the words pour out and ladle the pertinent stuff out. Took more time than straight conversation, but it worked.

The sound of Powderly's front door banging open startled us all.

"Deal me in, boys," Helen Anthony said. "I had me a good nap, and now I'm ready to clean your clocks."

She breezed in, wearing a flower print dress with a gauzy beige wrap over her bony shoulders. Her hair was piled on top of her head and held in place by a long pin with an ivory bead at the blunt end. The strong smell of a flower garden preceded her.

"Hey, Helen," Madison said. "About time you got here. This game's no fun with just two people playing."

"I don't see any money on the table," she said. "That's why it's no fun." She opened her purse and dumped a clump of wrinkled bills on the table. "Put some moolah in the pot, boys." She turned toward me and smiled broadly. "Hi there, you big hunk you; you find out yet what happened to Geraldine?"

"Don't pay Helen no mind," Powderly said as she pulled a chair up and sat down. "She's always hyper after her nap."

"Shut up and put some money on the table, Bill. What were you guys doing before I got here?"

"We were just telling Mr. Pennyback about the bad blood between Ms. Arden and the doctor."

She made a sound, somewhere between the grunt of a pig and the honk of a goose, her nostrils flaring.

"Them two fight like a married couple, and, I should know; they remind me of me and my third; or was it my fourth; husband. Fought like cats and dogs in public, but, boy, when we were behind closed doors."

"I don't think Ms. Arden and the doctor are doing anything like that," Madison said. "Especially not with that boyfriend of hers; he looks like he could break the doctor in half with one hand."

"Didn't say they were," Anthony said, sniffing again. "Just saying that's how me and my – whichever number; I had six, so sometimes they get mixed up in my mind – husband used to act." She looked at me; a twinkle in her eyes. "It's true, though, the two of them don't get along."

"Tell me, Ms. Anthony," I said. "Which one of them do you think would want to hurt your friend?"

"Call me Helen, hon," she said, fluttering her lashes at me. "That's hard to say really. Teresa Arden's a hardnosed bitch with a heart of granite. All she cares about is money and power. Dr. Winthrop has an ego the size of Texas, and I don't think he cares a whit about anyone but himself. Now, having said all that, I'm not sure I see either one of them trying to harm any of us who live here. We're their bread and butter, remember."

"Well, Arden is having money problems."

"Honey, who isn't? Don't see how hurting Geraldine would solve them, though, do you?"

"She controls the center's financial affairs. She could be siphoning off money there." I knew when I said it I was reaching, and so did Helen Anthony.

"She works for a board, and I imagine they audit this place's books from time to time. Don't see how she could be stealing and not get caught."

"Besides," Powderly said. "Geraldine didn't have all that much. I mean, she had a trust that was paying her upkeep here, and some jewelry and stuff, but nothing really worth killing for."

"And, her trust fund was getting pretty low," Anthony said. "She was probably gonna have to sell some of her jewelry to be able to keep making the payments here."

"Was her jewelry worth much?"

"She had a few old pieces that'd probably fetch a good price; I suppose in all maybe a hundred thousand dollars' worth."

Nothing worth killing for indeed, I thought. I've known people to kill for less than a hundred grand. I'd just about let Teresa Arden off the hook until that little bombshell was dropped.

"You don't think that's enough to get excited over?"

The all shrugged. I guess when you can afford to live in an exclusive place like Shady Grove, your definition of poverty and wealth is different from the average person.

"Okay, guys," I said. "You're not giving me much to go on. You're telling me you think your friend didn't die of a heart attack; at least not a natural one, if there is such a thing; but, the two people with motive and opportunity to do it, you don't think did it; am I right so far?"

Three heads bobbed in unison.

"You know you're making this an almost impossible case to solve."

"Well, of course," William Powderly said. "If it was easy we wouldn't have to hire you now would we?"

Chapter 23

Just as I got in my car to drive back to the office, Heather called. Quincy Chang wanted to see me at his office, and she said it was urgent. So, I took I-270 to River Road and then went into the District, making my way across town to K Street where Holcombe, Stein and Chang have their law offices.

Quincy had made arrangements for me to park my car in one of the two dozen spaces in the underground garage that were reserved for the firm, which meant I saved the seventy-five-buck fee for parking. An express elevator from the VIP parking went straight to the firm's floor.

The young receptionist in the front waved me down the corridor toward Quincy's office, and the blue-haired palace guard who'd been working as his personal assistant since he'd left the army and joined the firm as a junior partner, did her usual flirtation routine with me before letting me enter his office. The fact that she's in her late sixties never seems to dissuade her from offering to do physically impossible things with my body. Problem is, I never know whether or not she's kidding.

Quincy, who is three years younger than me, but looks ten with his third-generation Chinese-American slightly tan, completely unwrinkled complexion, shiny black hair without a trace of gray, and almond eyes with nary a trace of laugh lines, was sitting behind his desk. A thin folder lay open in front of him.

"Hey, Al," he said as I entered. "Thanks for coming so quickly. I know you're working on another case, but I've one that needs to be resolved immediately."

Holcombe, Stein and Chang pay me a retainer of ten thousand bucks a month, which comes to about five hundred a day, and, when I had extra expenses doing work for them, they paid the extra money without blinking. Therefore, if they wanted me to drop what I was doing for lower paying clients for a while, I'd be hard pressed to say no. Considering the lack of progress I was making on my current case, I was happy for the diversion.

"What do you need me to do?"

He lifted a sheet of paper from the folder, holding it gingerly. "I know you're busy on this case for those people at Shady Grove; Heather told me about it; but, I have a little errand I need you to run for me. It won't take more than a day, and it's really important."

"Does it have to be done today?"

"No, I don't think you'll have time to do it today. You see, it requires a couple hours' drive." He handed the sheet across to me. "We have this client, Angus Kentworthy, CEO of Kentworthy Trucking. He recently remarried, and unfortunately, he made the mistake of asking his new bride to sign an inheritance agreement *after* the wedding rather than a pre-nup. She got ticked off when he did it and went back home. Now, Angus has decided he'd rather have his trophy wife than worry about his estate. She won't return his calls, and he's reluctant to go to her, so he's written this letter and would like it delivered."

The one kind of case I avoid like poison ivy is a case involving a domestic dispute. I don't tail cheating spouses to get dirt for divorce cases, and I don't get between warring spouses. This was too close to that category for me.

"Couldn't you get one of your associates to deliver this? You know I don't do this kind of case."

"I thought about that, but considering where Ms. Kentworthy is, I thought it might be better if someone who could take care of himself did it. I know I'm imposing, Al, but all you have to do is deliver the letter, listen to what she has to say and come back and tell me so I can tell the client. Two hours down and two back, and maybe an hour on the ground. I'll add a thousand bucks to your retainer this month if you'll do it."

I did the arithmetic; five hours for a thousand bucks; two hundred per hour. Not bad for just delivering a letter; and we could use the extra money. Maybe I could go ahead and get Heather that color printer I'd seen her drooling over in one of the computer equipment catalogs she gets in the mail.

"Okay, but, I hope you don't make a habit of coming up with this kind of stuff," I said. "Where do I find the runaway bride?"

He took a gold Cross pen from his desk and wrote a name and address on a cream-colored piece of paper, and handed it to me. Millicent Slaughter Kentworthy, RFD 22, Dooms, Virginia, it read. I had no idea where Dooms was, and neither did Quincy.

"Maybe Heather can find it using one of those computer map search programs," he suggested.

I was sure she could; I just wasn't sure I wanted her to. But, I'd promised, so I'd do it. I called Heather and gave her the address. She put me on hold for five minutes.

"It's down U.S. 340," she said when she

came back on. "If you have a pen handy, I'll give you the best route."

I borrowed a piece of Quincy's fancy note paper, but stopped short of asking if I could use his fancy pen, opting to use my drug store-purchased ballpoint. Dooms, Heather said, could be reached by taking Lee Highway west toward New Market, and then south on U.S. 340 a few miles past Salem. Her map program didn't show the rural address, but she said the town was small, so I should be able to get directions to the house after I got there. I folded the directions with the name and address and put them in my pocket.

"Quince, old buddy," I said. "You owe me more than money for this."

"I know, pal. I'll buy you a case of *dos equis* tomorrow, how about that?"

"Make it two; this is down in the sticks, and you know how I hate being in the sticks." I love Mexican beer, and if he'd stuck to his guns I would have settled for one case. But, he caved.

"Okay, two cases."

My lucky day; a thousand bucks and two cases of primo Mexican *cerveza,* and, all for just playing mailman for a few hours.

"I'm just glad this client of yours didn't have one of those Russian mail order brides."

Chapter 24

The next morning, I called Heather from home and told her to keep digging on the Wallace case and to expect me to make it to the office after lunch. After exercising, meditating, and having a quiet breakfast with Sandra, I fired up the Mustang and headed south.

From River Road, I was able to get directly onto I-495, missing the snarled traffic on southbound I-270, but the bit of the Beltway I had to use to get to I-66 was jammed with morning commuters feeding in from the suburban communities of Montgomery County and Northern Virginia. From the Legion Bridge, over the Potomac, around to the I-66 exit ramp, the traffic averaged about 20 MPH, with the occasional jerk cutting to close in front of someone causing everyone to stand on their brakes and backing traffic up for miles. It took me 20 minutes to drive less than seven miles. Fortunately, most of the traffic on 66 was inbound, so I was quickly able to make up the lost time.

Just after Manassas National Battlefield Park, I exited onto Lee Highway, heading southwest toward Warrenton. Except for the few new housing developments, overpriced clones of the mansions you see in places like Potomac and McLean, the view alongside the road was rural; lots of rolling pastures with horses and a few cows, and gleaming white farm houses on hills with winding gravel drives up from the road.

The further south I drove the more rural it got, with more barns, some old and decrepit, antique shops, gun shops, and food stands being the main structures along the road. I passed through towns like Shenandoah, Elkton, Island Ford, and Orimora; some of them not even towns, but just collection of older frame houses on either side of the road, with an occasional gas station squatting on a concrete pad amidst ragged weeds breaking through the pavement. Not a few of the houses had broken down cars or pickups sitting on blocks in overgrown front yards.

About a mile from Dooms, I pulled into the parking lot of a duplex structure; the right hand one advertising antiques, jellies, jams and fresh fruits, and the right hand one selling guns of all calibers. I decided to try the antique shop.

A tall woman with hair the color of a pumpkin piled atop her head, light purple eye shadow, pink lipstick, and dark purple fingernails, with breasts that threatened to break free of her neon yellow blouse and hips that were straining dark green pants nearly to the breaking point, stood behind the counter just inside the door. She looked up, smiling, when I entered. There were three other customers; a middle aged man wearing overalls and a John Deere cap, and an elderly couple, the man being led around by the woman as if he was a two-year-old.

"Welcome to *Yesterday's Memories*," Pumpkin-top said. "If you don't see what you want, just ask; I guarantee we can get it. I highly recommend our strawberry preserves; they go well with pancakes."

I was tempted, but decided to maybe stop on my way back to DC. "Thanks, but I'm trying to find someone in the town of Dooms, and I thought you might be able to help."

"Well, hon, first of all, Dooms ain't hardly a town. It's just a collection of houses and a couple churches. Its only claim to fame is the big purple cow head. Who you looking for?"

"Millicent Kentworthy."

"I know just about everybody in these parts, and there ain't no Kentworthys," she said. "You sure you got the name right?"

"Sorry; her maiden name is Slaughter."

"Oh, why didn't you say so in the first place? 'Course I know Millie Slaughter. Her and her sister Diana live on their folks' farm just east of the highway." She pulled a sheet of paper from beneath the counter. "Here, I'll draw you a map of how to get there."

The directions seemed straightforward. I thanked her and told her I'd stop and look at her jellies on my way back. She leaned forward and let me know her jelly wasn't the only thing I'd be welcome to look at. The guy with the John Deere cap gave me a dirty look as I passed him on the way out.

Chapter 25

The redhead counter woman's directions were good. And, she'd been right; Dooms was no longer a town, if indeed it ever had been. There were houses on both sides of the highway; an assortment of modest frame houses, some with well-kept lawns, some with scraggly weeds and packed clay; a few one-story buildings that looked like they might at one time been cafes or small stores, but were now vacant, and I could see the steeples of two churches just beyond the road she said I should turn on. I also saw the big purple cow head atop a scaffold outside a vacant building that still had fliers or posters stuck in the windows, but looked as if it hadn't been used in some time.

The road ran straight for about a mile, but when the macadam turned to mainly gravel, it began to curve uphill, and was lined on both sides with large hardwood trees and a broken down wooden fence.

Near the top of the gentle rise, the road curved right and then straightened out, aimed like a spear at a large white house with a wraparound verandah with columns that stretched up to the second floor. In the distance I could see four people standing on the verandah watching my approach. As I got closer, the four figures resolved into two women, dressed similarly in white blouses and jeans, and two men; one was the guy I'd seen in the jelly shop, still wearing his John Deere cap, and the other, dressed in overalls with one of the shoulder straps hanging loose, was thin and young. His lank brown hair, which hung down over his brows, failed to hide the acne scars on his cheeks and brow, which were visible even through my front window from twenty feet away. The frowns on all their faces were also plainly visible.

I braked about ten feet from the verandah and turned the engine off. As I got out of the car, the taller of the two women, a striking blonde with high cheekbones and a sharp nose, stepped down to the bottom of the steps.

"This the fella you were tellin' us about, Jake?" she asked the older man.

"Yup, that's him. Told Mabel he was lookin' for Millicent Slaughter. I done heard him plain as day." He stepped off the verandah to stand beside her. The young man stepped down and took up a position on her other side. The other woman, a thin-faced girl really, with lank brown hair that looked like a twin of the younger man, stayed on the verandah.

"What you want, stranger?" the blonde asked.

I didn't see any weapons, but I was in gun country, so I moved slowly. I removed my ID from my pocket and held it up so she could see. "My name's Al Pennyback. I work for a law firm in DC, and I have a document to be delivered to Millicent Slaughter Kentworthy."

"What kind of document?"

"It's a private communication that I should really deliver only to the named recipient."

She put her hands on shapely hips and looked at me as if I'd just dropped from the hinter regions of a dog. "We Slaughters don't have no secrets from each other. You got something, you just hand it over."

"If you insist, but I'll have wait until it's read and take a response back to the sender."

She frowned and the hands on her hips balled into fists. The older man stepped forward.

"You'll jest hand over that there letter and git your carcass back on the road is what you gone do, boy."

He glared at me, his hands balled into fists and held aggressively. I looked at him evenly, standing relaxed, with my hands at my side. "I don't know how long childhood lasts where you come from, friend, but I haven't been a boy for a few decades now. I owe my employer an answer, and I'm staying here until I get it."

"Oh yeah, well I think your smart ass needs a proper whupping to teach you your place. Henry, come on down here and lets us teach this boy a lesson in manners."

The skinny one sauntered down the steps, a leer on his acne-ravaged face. The two of them approached me, the older man to my left and a step or two in front of his young accomplice. The blonde stood her ground, smiling expectantly, while the younger woman stood on the verandah, her hands over her mouth and her eyes wide.

The two men stopped about five feet from me. The older man had his fists clenched at his side, his left foot slightly forward and was poised on the balls of his feet. He'd either boxed or done a lot of street fighting. The bump in his nose and the lines around his eyes indicated that he'd been punched in the face a lot of times. Acne-boy stood flat footed with his hands hooked into the flap of his overalls with a smirk on his face.

"Look, fellas," I said. "I'm not here looking for trouble. I have a job to do, and I'm just trying to do it. Now, you can do it the easy way and let me *do* my job, or we can do it the hard way and someone's gonna get hurt."

"Well now, if you don't want to git hurt, jest hand over the paper and haul your ass outta here," the older guy, Jake, said.

"If I was you, mister," the blonde said. "I'd do what he says. Cousin Jake's the best fighter 'round these parts. He done put more than one guy in the hospital."

The grin on his lined and scarred face said he'd enjoy doing just that. "Just take the letter, read it, and give me your reaction to it, and I'm out of here. It's that simple."

"Life's not simple," she said. "You're on private property, and we got a right to defend it. If you don't hand over the document and leave, I'm afraid Jake and Henry will have to forcefully evict you."

"Sorry, lady; I can't do that."

"Well, boys, you heard the man. Seems like he's the one who wants to do it the hard way."

Jake, the older man, started his forward lunge, his right fist coming up from waist level. The younger one was a beat slower moving.

I slid to my left, putting the bulk of Jake's

body between me and his companion and blocked the uppercut in the crook of my left thumb and index finger. At the same time I hit him in the Adam's apple with the crook of my right thumb and index finger, not hard enough to crush his larynx, but hard enough to hurt like hell. He gagged and bent forward, reaching for his throat with his left hand. I released his right hand and slammed the knuckles of my left hand against his temple. He groaned and made a gurgling sound and began sagging.

I then grabbed the front of his shirt and pushed him around and against Henry, who was just beginning to bring his own fists up. As he splayed his hands out to brace himself against the force of the heavier man's body I snapped a jab to the point of his chin with my right hand, stepped back a pace and swiveled, bringing my left foot up and snap-kicked his crotch. He made a squealing sound that sounded like a hungry kitten, grabbing for his chin and crotch at the same time.

As he jackknifed forward, I pulled my right hand back and swung from my waist, catching him on the chin, snapping his head back. His eyes rolled up and he kept falling backwards like a small tree, landing with a dull thud and laying still.

Jake was just beginning to get some wind into his lungs and started to straighten. As he raised his upper body and started turning toward me, I rammed the stiffened fingers of my right hand into his sternum, knocking what little air he'd sucked in right back out. I then went into a fighter's crouch and hit him with a one-two; left jab to the chin and a right cross that knocked his head to the right and sent him sprawling. He too lay still. I turned to the blonde.

"Like I said, if we do it the hard way, someone's gonna get hurt. You ready to take the document now?"

She smiled. "Looks like Cousin Jake's no longer the best fighter in these parts. Okay, hand it over, friend."

I took the folder letter from my pocket and shoved it toward her. She shook her head. "It ain't for me. I'm Diana. You said it was for Millicent." She looked back over her shoulder at the girl on the verandah. "Get on down here, girl and see what the man done brought you."

Chapter 26

The girl, who didn't look more than fifteen, came down the steps, walking like a condemned prisoner on the way to the gallows. She stopped about an arm's length from me and reached out a tiny hand. Her hand trembled.

"This from Angus?" she asked in a small voice that was barely audible.

I hesitated. "This is written to his wife." I looked from her to the blonde. The blonde smiled.

"That's Millicent all right," she said. "I know what's goin' through your mind. She don't hardly look growed up, but she's nineteen, and she did marry that Angus Kentworthy fella."

I handed the girl the paper. She unfolded it and began reading it, her lips moving. She then looked at me, an imploring expression in her eyes. "This really come from Angus?"

"I got it from his lawyer, but I trust him; so, I'd say it did."

She turned to the blonde. "He says he apologizes for that paper he wanted me to sign, and if I come back, he'll never bring it up again. What should I do, Diana?"

"Well, girl, I guess the question you gotta ask is, do you love him?"

"He's okay. 'Cept for askin' me to sign that paper sayin' I wouldn't try to get his money, he treated me nice."

"That don't answer my question, but I reckon comin' from you that's as close as it's gonna git. I reckon that means you goin' back to him."

The girl played idly with a lank tress, putting the end into her mouth. Then, she took it out and looked at me. "I reckon you can tell him I'll be comin' back."

"Well, there you have it," the blonde said. "You delivered your letter and you got your message to take back. Guess you done earned your pay today."

I guess I had; but, I thought, I should have held out for three cases of beer and an extra five thousand. I nodded and turned to leave. The older man began to stir. I tensed.

"Don't worry 'bout him, mister," the blonde

said. "You done knocked all the fight out of him. 'Sides, I wouldn't let him do no more. I need him to do chores 'round here, and I'm 'fraid if he goes at you again, he might be stove up too long."

Something in the matter of fact tone of her voice reassured me. Jake might be an alpha male, but she was clearly the leader of this pack. I nodded again and got into my car. As I did a three point turn to leave, Jake was sitting up, rubbing at his temple and looking confused. Henry was just beginning to stir.

The blonde was standing over them, her legs apart and her hands on her hips, staring after me.

I stopped at the redhead's shop and bought a jar each of strawberry and black currant jelly, some peach preserves, and a bottle of maple syrup. The redhead had unbuttoned the top two buttons of her blouse, and let me look at her other fruits as I perused the selection of condiments.

Chapter 27

It was nearly four by the time I got to the office.

I breezed past Heather and headed for my office.

"Boss, I've some new information on the Shady Grove case," she said.

"Okay, let me call Quince first, then come in and give it to me," I said.

She grabbed a note pad and a stack of papers from her desk and followed me into my office.

When I got Quincy on the phone and gave him a report of my trip to Dooms, Heather's eyes got all round.

"I'll pass the message to Angus," Quincy said. "Thanks, Al. I owe you big time for this."

"You got that right, pal," I said. "I feel like an

accessory to cradle robbing getting those two back together."

"Hey, she's legal age; and, it's a symbiotic relationship. She's got few prospects of finding a husband down there in the sticks, and he'll have someone to change his diaper when he needs it."

"All the same, I hope you don't have any more geriatric clients needing help hooking up."

He was laughing as he broke the connection. Heather was sitting there, her mouth open, and her note pad open on her lap.

"You're kidding, right?" she asked. "Some old codger sent you to the countryside to retrieve his teenage bride?"

I shrugged. "Yeah, and I had to beat up two of her cousins to do it."

She rolled her eyes and shook her head, her blonde hair waving back and forth. "Only you can get into situations like this."

"Well, at least I got some good jelly and two cases of Mexican beer in the bargain; and, the extra money almost makes up for it. Reminds me; how'd you like a jar of black currant jelly?"

"Hmph, so that's my bonus for this job? Better than nothing, I suppose. Before I forget, I found some more information about the people at Shady Grove that I think you'll find interesting."

"You got some proof that Winthrop's made some bad medical calls in the past?"

"No, but I did learn something interesting about Wilomena Dunn." She took a sheet from the stack of papers and passed it to me.

It was a black and white print, downloaded no doubt from some Internet site Heather had found. It was dark, but the faces in the picture were clear enough, and what I saw was interesting.

It was a candid photo of the students of an obscure nursing school; six women in nurses' whites sitting around a table with smiles on their faces. The two figures in the center, though, were what interested me. There, holding hands and smiling at each other were Wilomena Dunn and Teresa Arden.

As I'd done with Millicent Kentworthy, I'd been looking in the wrong direction all along. Wilomena Dunn, the mousy, quiet little nurse, hadn't come up on my radar once during the investigation. I'd considered her no more than supporting cast, the nameless, faceless players who stand in the background and serve mainly as props and foils for the lead actors. It had never occurred to me, even after learning that Arden had attended nursing school, to link the two women. As a consequence, I'd not questioned Dunn all that closely. I'd thought of her merely as Winthrop's assistant, at his beck and call, and under his observation and supervision. I then remembered what I'd been told; in nursing homes, it's often the nurse who pronounces the death of a patient, and the physician just signs the papers.

I needed to rectify that little oversight.

Chapter 28

The next morning, I called Heather at the office and let her know that I'd be going first to Shady Grove.

Wilomena Dunn wasn't in her office when I arrived. When I went back to reception and asked, the young guy on duty said that it she wasn't in her office, she'd probably be in the clinic which was just next door. He then said there was a door from her office directly into the clinic to enable her to get back and forth easily to see patients.

I found her with a patient in the clinic. The elderly woman was just buttoning her blouse when I walked in.

"You really shouldn't come in here while I'm seeing a patient," she said.

"Sorry," I said. "I didn't know you had a patient. I'll wait for you in your office." I looked around and saw the door to the left side of the clinic. I walked toward it.

"No need to apologize, honey," the old woman said. "I ain't got nothing to be ashamed of. Shoot, it's been a long time since a man eyeballed my goodies."

I laughed. Dunn glared at me.

"Mrs. Tatum, you should be ashamed of your language," she said.

The old lady laughed. "Well, sorry, sweetie, but I'm not." She swayed her narrow hips suggestively as she exited.

Dunn shook her head. "Now, Mr. Pennyback, let's go to my office. You really shouldn't even be in here." She picked up a green folder and headed toward the door.

I stepped aside and let her go through the door, and then followed. Inside her office, I could see how I'd missed the door. It didn't have a knob on her side, she just pushed it inward, and when closed it sat so flush with the wall it would only be seen by peering closely at it.

"So, you have a way to get into and out of the clinic without having to go into the hallway I see."

"Well, yes," she said. "It's convenient when I have patients coming in at irregular intervals. There's a bell at the front, and when they ring it, I just pop over and see what they want."

"Dr. Winthrop's office is on the other side of the clinic; does he have a direct door as well?"

"Why, yes. Wouldn't do to have him running back and forth in the hallway."

I sat in the chair next to her desk without waiting for her to sit. She made some notes in the folder and put it in the cabinet behind her desk.

"Doesn't the doctor have to see people when they come to the clinic?" I asked.

She shook her head. "For serious things, he does. I take care of the routine aches and pains. For most of our residents, it only requires an aspirin, a laxative, or some liniment."

"So, the day Geraldine Wallace came in, who saw her first, you or the doctor?"

She looked down at the desk and started drumming her fingers on the desk.

"Which one of us saw her first? Well, I guess I probably did. Uh, yes, now that I recall; when she rang the bell I went in and talked to her."

"What happened after you talked to her?"

"What happened? She said her stomach was upset and she had heartburn. Uh, and then, I gave her an antacid. But, it didn't help. After ten minutes she said she was stilling discomfort in her chest. I, uh, then I took her blood pressure and pulse and noticed that both were elevated, so I called Dr. Winthrop."

"So; you were alone with her for fifteen minutes?"

"Yes, more or less. Why do you ask?"

I leaned forward, placing my hand next to hers on the desk. "When I asked you to tell me everything that happened that day, you left that part out."

"What part?"

"The part about your being alone with her before the doctor examined her."

Her eyebrows shot up. "Oh, well, I didn't think of it. I mean, I'm with every patient before the doctor unless it's after hours and he's the one on duty. And, I'm with every female patient while they undress and dress. That's our standard procedure. I guess it just slipped my mind. Why is it important anyway?"

She had her chin tucked in, looking at me from beneath her brows, and was shrinking back in her chair. Maybe it was because I felt foolish for having overlooked her; maybe because she was acting guilty and I could smell her fear; but, I decided to play hardball with her to see what happened.

"It's important because I'm convinced that

something other than a simple heart attack that killed Geraldine Wallace, and anyone who was alone with her had the opportunity to kill her."

Her mouth snapped shut, opened, and shut again. "Y-you, you can't be suggesting that I killed poor Ms. Wallace."

"Maybe not deliberately; but, it's possible that one of you gave her something that caused a nasty reaction. You know, the doctor misdiagnosed her, or you gave her something to ease her reported indigestion?"

"T-that's ridiculous. I don't think Dr. Winthrop misdiagnosed. It was a heart attack. Why on earth would either of us want to harm her?"

She had me there. She had the means and opportunity, of that I was certain, but, I couldn't see her motive. And, even with her skittishness, she didn't appear to be ready to confess. I was in a corner. But, I'd become certain, as certain as I could be, that Wilomena Dunn was the perpetrator.

"I'm still working on that," I said. "Just so you know; I'm pretty certain that something you did was responsible for Geraldine Wallace's death, and I don't plan to rest until I prove it."

Her eyes glistened with unshed tears, and her hands trembled. But, her face was like marble. She knew I couldn't pin anything definite on her. "Good luck doing that," she said.

Chapter 29

Luck didn't have anything to do with it; well, not much at least.

Pinning Ms. Dunn to the wall would be a matter of finding out what made her tick. I had loose ends to tie up and entanglements to unsnarl, and one of the ends that came to mind was the relationship between Wilomena Dunn and Teresa Arden. I found it interesting that neither of them had bothered to mention that they were acquainted prior to coming to their current positions.

I made my way down the hallway to Arden's office. She was sitting behind her desk, her back to the door and her feet on the shelf of a bookcase behind her. At the sound of her door opening, she whirled around.

"Well, if it isn't the intrepid investigator," she said. "Back to follow some new lead?"

I sat down. "Yes, I'm here to follow a new lead. I'm trying to figure out why you've been withholding information from me."

"I told you about going to nursing school; sure, I should have mentioned it the first time, but I didn't think it mattered. There's nothing else I haven't told you."

She either had a very selective memory, or she thought I didn't know, and couldn't find out, more about her background. Nothing in her body language or tone of voice, though, indicated she was deliberately lying.

"Now, now, Ms. Arden," I said. "Don't you think you relationship with the center's nurse is important to this case?"

She leaned back in her chair, her eyes widening slightly. "Uh, Wilomena and I don't have a *relationship.*"

"But, you knew each other before coming to work here."

She opened her mouth in a little circle, and then closed it, puffing out her cheeks.

"Ah, oh, that; uh, yes, she and I were in nursing school together; but, for less than a year. She started when I was in my third year, and I quit just before graduation, when I realized that I just wasn't cut out to be a nurse."

"So, you're telling me that you two didn't know each other well in school? That you haven't renewed your old friendship now that you're working together here?"

You hear it said that a person's inner emotions are reflected in their face, but, until that moment I'd never appreciated the meaning of that statement. A storm of conflicting emotions clouded her face. She seemed torn between anger and embarrassment.

Finally, she took a deep breath and let it out slowly, regarding me with a steady gaze.

"Okay, we did know each other in nursing school. Wilomena was, is, the clinging type, and for some reason, she latched onto me from the first day. She's such a mild mannered person, you can't help but like her; or maybe it's just you feel sorry for her."

"You had a close friendship?"

"At first, I guess you could say that. I mean, she followed me around like a little puppy, always wanting to do things for me. I don't think she'd ever had a close friend before. Anyway, that's all it was for the first couple of months. Then, it got sort of weird. She got too touchy feely if you know what I mean. It was never anything direct, but it creeped me out, so I tried to put some distance between us, and then just over halfway through the year, I came to my senses and realized that I wasn't cut out to be a nurse. I left nursing school. I was working here before she came. I guess you could say we're still friends." She shrugged. "I mean, technically, I'm her boss, and I don't get too many chances to talk to her."

She leaned forward, her breasts pushing against the edge of her desk.

"She doesn't talk that much to anyone here for that matter," she continued. "Like that night Ms. Wallace died. Wilomena was in the dining room. She sort of waved at us when she came in, but she got her food and sat alone at a table in the corner instead of joining us. I remember going over and offering her a piece of my cake, and she turned me down. I mean, she wasn't unfriendly or anything, more like she was shy or afraid."

"What's her relationship with Morgan Winthrop?"

"Well, for starters, Morgan's no Dr. Kildare. I imagine it's an 'I'm the doctor, you're the nurse; do what I tell you and shut up' kind of relationship. And, Wilomena's such a submissive personality, she'd just take it."

"Is he the abusive type?"

She laughed. "I assume you mean verbally abusive. He's the stereotype of the arrogant doctor who thinks everyone else is inferior. Yeah, I'd say he's verbally abusive; not in a loud or profane way, but subtly, quietly."

A loose end was starting to resolve itself into a nice bow. I didn't agree totally with Arden that the mousy little nurse would just 'take' abusive behavior. What usually passes for reticence and shyness in many people is in reality just passive-aggressive behavior. The guy or gal who seems to be meekly submitting to your aggression is often quietly plotting an act of revenge that is designed to make your malefaction look mild by comparison.

Wilomena Dunn had the means and more than ample opportunity, and I was beginning to see the faint outlines of motive.

The noose was tightening.

Chapter 30

My next stop was Morgan Winthrop's office. He seemed less than happy to see me.

"Mr. Pennyback," he said. "I thought you and I had had our last conversation. I really have nothing else to say to you."

He looked at me down the length of his nose.

"Look, doc," I said. "I think we got off on the wrong foot. I know I was maybe a little out of line with some of the things I said, and I'm here to apologize."

He looked at me and blinked. The elevated nose dipped a few degrees. Nothing like massaging the ego a little to soften people up; and, to get the information I sought, I was prepared to ladle it on thick.

"Ah, well, I see," he said. "Well, of course; I guess you were just trying to do the job you've been hired to do. I can understand that.

Perhaps I was overreacting to your approach."

I felt it then.

That little twinge of excitement and anticipation a fisherman gets when, after putting his lure into the water, he feels that first tug signaling that his prey has taken the bait. That's a critical moment. For the inexperienced there's a temptation to immediately try to haul the catch in. But, that would be a mistake. Quite often, that first tug is just a sign that the prey is testing; tasting the bait to determine whether or not it's worth going for. The key to catching the big ones is to let those first samplings play themselves out; let the target become comfortable in the knowledge that he's the hunter rather than the hunted until he's firmly hooked.

"No," I said. "Your reaction was completely justified. I guess I was so determined to deliver the goods to my client, I struck out blindly. I should have known better. It was rash of me to assume that a doctor of your skill and experience would make such a mistake."

I could sense that he was taking the bait. His features relaxed, and his expression of self-satisfied superiority was beginning to reassert itself.

"Yes, I can understand how a lay person would be confused. But, let me assure you; Geraldine Wallace did indeed suffer a massive coronary." It was the first time he'd referred to her as something other than 'the patient.' "It's distressing to lose a patient, but one has to accept that not everyone can be saved. In her case, poor diet and advanced age worked against us."

"I'm sure you did all you could possibly do. But, tell me; was she under your observation for the entire time?"

"Yes, for the most part. I mean, the nurse, of course, checked her in and took the preliminary readings before calling me."

"And, you came in immediately? Like the nurse, your office has an adjoining door, right?"

"Yes, it does; and, yes, I came in . . . well, I was on an important call, and had to complete it, but it was only a matter of a few minutes."

"Could you do me a favor, doctor; could you walk me through what happened that day? Just so I have a better understanding, and don't go shooting my mouth off about things again."

The bait was firmly between his teeth. I didn't have to pull too hard; he began reeling himself in.

He described how, after completing his phone call, he'd come in and found Geraldine sitting on the examination table, already in one of those backless paper gowns they make you wear when they poke and prod you. She was complaining of chest pains, difficulty breathing, and numbness in her arms, particularly the left arm. Dunn showed him the blood pressure readings and informed him that she'd given the patient an antacid which hadn't relieved the symptoms. He had, he said, begun to immediately suspect that it was something more serious than indigestion and ordered Dunn to prepare for an ECG. As he was scrubbing, Wallace went into convulsions, and then passed out. At first, her blood pressure was off the chart, but then, her heart stopped. Working with Dunn, he'd tried to resuscitate her, to no avail.

"There was no heartbeat for five or ten minutes – you have to understand, under the circumstances I wasn't exactly looking at my watch that much. After that long with no blood being pumped to her brain, though, she would probably have suffered irreversible brain damage even if we'd been able to bring her back."

I knew enough about medicine to know that he was right. But, what had interested me was that Dunn had been alone with the patient for a while before he came in, and, more importantly, when he was washing his hands, he would have had his back to both.

Now, all I had to do was establish Dunn's motive for the murder of Geraldine Wallace.

Chapter 31

I went to the office with almost all of the puzzle pieces in place.

It was just left to find that final, crucial part; that little piece of solid blue that fills in the sky and makes the puzzle whole. But, like the blue piece that seems to always be missing from a jigsaw puzzle, finding it wouldn't be easy.

I didn't think a simple 'bait in the water' would attract Wilomena Dunn from her hiding place.

When I entered the office, Heather was at her desk, her fingers making clicking sounds on her computer keyboard, the screen flickering in response to her strokes, a secretary's notebook; one of those rectangular kind with the metal spirals holding the lined paper together between stiff white covers; open at the side of the keyboard, a cup of tea at the other side, smelling like the bargain section of a florist.

"Hey, boss," she said, looking up with a cheerful expression. "How'd things go at the center?"

I told her my suspicions, and what Winthrop had said about the events of the fateful evening.

"So, this nurse, Wilomena Dunn, was alone with poor Ms. Wallace long enough to have given her something," she said. "But, why would she do it? Was there a history between them? I don't think so; I've checked that place from attic to basement, and as far as I can see, none of the staff have had any problems with any of the residents."

"I think it's more complex than that," I said. Then, I remembered the message Blood Raine had sent via Elizabeth Sung. "I don't think it really had anything to do with Geraldine Wallace."

"Whoa, boss! You're going to have to explain that one slowly. She was the one killed; how could it not have anything to do with her?"

"I'm not sure I *can* explain it. It's more a strong hunch; but, I'm fairly convinced that Dunn's the perpetrator. I think there's something else that served as a trigger for what she did; nothing to do with Wallace other than her convenient presence."

"That's too deep for me." Then, she reached down and started flipping the pages of her notebook. "But, wait . . . there was something I stumbled across now that I think of it. Where was that . . ., oh yeah, here it is."

She'd reached a page that was filled with her neat handwriting. She ran her finger down the page.

"Yes, here are my notes from a phone conversation I had with a woman who was in nursing school the same time as both Dunn and Arden. I didn't think much of it at the time, but it was strange enough, I wrote it all down. Teresa Arden was a couple years ahead of Wilomena Dunn, but when Wilomena enrolled they became friends. According to this woman, it was a very close friendship, with Teresa in the dominant role. She said Wilomena followed her around like a little puppy, always at her beck and call. Teresa didn't drop out of nursing call, by the way; she was asked to leave, and that broke Wilomena up."

"What do you mean, she was asked to leave? She indicated to me that she left because she realized she wasn't cut out to be a nurse."

"Hah! That's not what the records show. I checked the woman's story against the school's records, by the way, and they agree. Teresa Arden was dismissed from the school. There were a number of reasons; but, mainly it had to do with her getting caught cutting corners on some examination or other. When the instructor confronted her about it, Teresa became verbally abusive. She was put on probation, but a few weeks later, she was found cheating on another test, and they gave her the boot."

"How does Wilomena figure into this?"

"I couldn't find anything in the records, but the woman who called said that Wilomena blamed the instructor for Teresa being kicked out of school and she slit the woman's tires. No one could ever prove it, but this woman said she saw it happen. She didn't turn Wilomena in because the particular instructor wasn't all that popular with the student body and she figures she deserved it."

Like a pet dog that bites anyone threatening its master. Wilomena Dunn was a complex personality; complex and dangerous. She would have to be handled with extreme care, but handled she'd have to be.

"Here's another interesting fact," Heather said, flipping back toward the front of her notebook. "You know those other deaths at the center; the ones of people who'd been otherwise healthy; well, at least two of them coincide with situations where Teresa Arden had had problems. In one case, there'd been a shortage in the accounts and she'd been under the gun for it; and in another, her boyfriend had made a scene at the center; threatening her and being abusive."

"So, Wilomena has herself cast in the role of Teresa's protector, only, she doesn't strike at the one threatening her directly. Sounds psychotic to me."

"The woman who called didn't exactly use that word; but, when she described Wilomena's actions after Teresa was kicked out of school, I got goose bumps. She said, if she had the power to make such decisions, she'd never let Wilomena Dunn near a patient. I think her exact words were, 'the girl has several screws loose.'

I didn't get goose bumps, but there was a cold feeling I the pit of my stomach. What Heather was describing was nothing less than a serial killer. And, probably one of the most dangerous kinds; one who to all outward appearances was harmless, even helpful; who is triggered to kill by events that seem totally external to them. But for Heather's digging, and her penchant for collecting even the most obscure snippet of information, it would never have occurred to me to link things happening to one person to the actions of another.

I was pretty certain at this point that a thorough investigation of deaths at the center would show that a number of them coincided with difficulties experienced by its director. Not exactly something that would occur to cops looking into suspicious deaths; wouldn't have occurred to yours truly, in fact. And, the connection would be damned hard to prove.

But, it also gave me an idea of the 'bait' that would lure Wilomena out of the dark mental cave into which she'd crawled, if indeed she hadn't been there her entire life.

I called Buster and asked him to run some interference for me with the local cops, telling him my suspicions and trusting him to provide an appropriately edited version to the police in Maryland. Then, I called Blood Raine and asked if I could come out to his place and look at some of his toys.

Chapter 32

The next morning, I set out bright and early for Shady Grove. As I made the last turn before the entrance to the center's grounds, I saw the unmarked Montgomery County police car, parked a block from the opening, two men in dark suits sitting in the front seat. They affected to ignore me as I drove past, but I saw one duck his head to speak into the small radio under his jacket.

I patted the thin brown jacket I wore. The device I'd borrowed from Blood could barely be felt; it was like a raised welt on my skin. In fact, it somewhat resembled a welt; a flat brown strip with little bumps, about ten inches long and an inch wide. It was only a few millimeters thick except at one end where a round hump concealed the nickel-cadmium battery that powered it. It was taped just under my sternum, and from the demonstration Blood had given when he loaned it to me, I knew the receiver in the cop car was thumping to the sound of my heart. Blood hadn't told me everything the device was capable of, just that it would suffice to record a conversation in close proximity, and with sufficient fidelity as to enable voice print identification. Another of his agency toys that his former colleagues let him have to 'field test.'

I parked next to Winthrop's space again; not bothering this time to worry about my car being close enough to ding his – after all, he and I had become friends. I breezed past the receptionist and went to Teresa Arden's office.

"Hi, back again," she said. "If I didn't know better, I'd say you were showing a greater interest in me than your case."

Under better circumstances, and if I hadn't already been in a relationship, that might be true.

"Actually," I said. "I'm here to solve a murder."

Her face creased in disappointment. I guess she hadn't been kidding; maybe her Canadian boy toy had ceased to amuse her, or maybe she was getting tired of his north woods' vulgarity.

"So, you think Geraldine Wallace was murdered?"

"I don't *think*, I know; and, if you'll come with me I'll tell you who the killer is."

She pursed her lips, but rose and followed me as I walked out the door and turned toward Morgan Winthrop's office.

"So, it was the good doctor after all?" There was a sound of almost glee in her voice.

"Not yet," I said. "All in good time."

Winthrop looked surprised, but when I told him I'd discovered the name of Geraldine Wallace's killer, and was prepared to expose that person, he rose and followed us.

Our next stop was Wilomena Dunn's office. She was sitting behind her desk, looking at patient files. She looked up in annoyance when the three of us trooped in.

"What - -"

I held up my hand to silence her.

"Come with us," I said. "In the clinic I will show all of you what happened to poor Geraldine Dunn."

Her eyes widened and her cheeks paled, but she rose. I pushed the door to the clinic open and walked through. I turned and rested my hips on the examination table as the three of them trailed in behind me and stood in a row in front of me; varying shades of confusion on their faces.

Morgan Winthrop was the first to break the

silence. "Okay, we're here; now what's all this about?"

I'm not normally given to theatrical displays, but there was something about the whole scene that evoked images of some grainy black and white movie when the detective has the cops and the family all lined up in the living room and with sweeping gestures unveils the culprit, showing how it was the butler who did it all along. Or, maybe the devil made me do it.

"Ladies and gentleman," I said. "What we have here is murder most foul."

The three gasped in unison. Wilomena's hand flew to her throat. Teresa's eyes went wide in shock. Morgan Winthrop looked at me as if he'd like to write a referral to a shrink.

"Come now," he said. "I thought we went through that. You agreed yesterday that my diagnosis wasn't incorrect."

"Well, doctor, I did and I didn't. I agreed that I'd been rash in accusing you of incompetence. I didn't say, though, that you'd been absolutely correct in your diagnosis."

He shook his head. "You can't have it both ways. I was either right, or I was wrong."

"Okay, let me try and explain it so you'll understand it. You were, I think, right that it was a heart attack. You were wrong, though, in thinking it was from natural causes."

Dunn's face drained of color, while Arden's went red. Winthrop's mouth dropped open.

"Y-you're saying she was poisoned? Who would do such a thing?"

"Before we get to the who; let's talk about the how and why. It puzzled me at first, you know; I mean, woman comes into the clinic complaining about indigestion and then has a massive heart attack, and as good as you are, doctor, you missed it. Well, that was because she in fact did have a heart attack. But, it was brought on in a most unnatural way."

His eyebrows arched upwards, the right one a fraction higher than the left.

"You see," I continued. "Her heart attack was brought on by the reaction of two substances in her system; substances that were introduced just for that purpose."

I slid slightly to the right, placing myself in front of Teresa Arden. Winthrop was to her right; and Dunn to his right. She stared at me, as did the two others.

"It was known that when these two substances came together in her body, they'd cause her heart to pound and her blood pressure would rise to dangerous levels, levels which, in someone her age, would most likely be fatal. The one who did this relied on you diagnosing what you saw and not questioning it." He opened his mouth, but I made a placating gesture. "You're not to be blamed, doctor. Anyone else would have done the same. That was the beauty of it, see. You'd see the patient suffering a heart attack; call it as you saw it, and the way the system works, that would be the end of it. It's really quite an elegant plot when you think about it."

Arden regarded me levelly. "You're not trying to revive your theory that I was the one who did it, are you?"

"Let's not get ahead of ourselves," I said. "There's more to the story, and you have to hear the whole thing." I returned her gaze. "You do have motive; you must admit. You're on the verge of bankruptcy. The need for money is a strong motivation for murder." She frowned and her brow furrowed. "But, that still leaves the problem of access. That one had me stumped for the longest time."

"But, I didn't have access. I never entered the clinic that evening."

"That's right," Winthrop said. "I don't recall seeing her anywhere near the clinic that day at all."

She gave him a strange look. His defense must have surprised her.

"Just because you didn't see her, doesn't mean she wasn't around, and, she did give

Wallace the chocolate cake in the dining room that evening."

He gave her a querying look. Her face colored.

"I've already told you; I didn't *offer* her the cake, she asked for it. My offer was to Bill Powderly. He is, as you well know, Morgan, the ring leader of those who fight against center rules and policies."

Winthrop nodded. Apparently, he too had had encounters with Powderly's stubbornness. "True; I've never been able to get him to follow any of my health recommendations; that is, when I can even get him to come in for an examination. Mr. Pennyback, you haven't said anything that would make me believe Teresa had anything to do with Ms. Wallace's ailment. She couldn't have known that chocolate would cause problems when mixed with some other medication. That takes medical knowledge."

"You mean you didn't know that Ms. Arden almost graduated from nursing school?"

His eyes widened, and he turned on her. "No, I did not know that. Teresa, you never mentioned that to me at any time."

"I didn't because it was of no concern. I dropped out of school before graduating and got my degree in business. But, what does that have to do with this?"

I raised a finger like a teacher making a point. "It means that you do have the medical knowledge to be aware of how chocolate, and the other things Geraldine Wallace ate that evening, would react if someone gave her an anti-depressant. And, you also neglected to mention that you didn't *drop out* of nursing school; you were expelled for cheating."

Her face reddened and her eyes glistened. "That was a total frame up. The teacher I'd had a run-in with had it in for me, and cooked that up to get rid of me. And, for the record, I wasn't expelled; I was asked to withdraw, and I did." She looked at Dunn. "You tell him, Wilomena. That old bitch was out to get me from the day we argued over that case study we were doing."

Dunn looked down at the floor. "Uh, that's true," she said almost inaudibly.

"You two were in nursing school together?" Winthrop asked.

"Yes, Wilomena enrolled during my last year. We had several classes together."

Now was the time for me to play my hole card. It was a long shot.

"None of that matters," I said. "What does is that you had the means and motive, and I believe you had the opportunity."

"W-what? What are you saying?" Her face was bright red now, and she was breathing heavily. "You can't be saying you think I killed her!"

"But, I am. Teresa Arden; I'm saying that in an effort to get your hands on the proceeds from Geraldine Wallace's estate, or at least a portion of it, you fed her chocolate, and then later somehow introduced another chemical into her system that you knew would cause a heart attack. You relied on Dr. Winthrop's habit of making a firm diagnosis and acting on it; knowing that his finding wouldn't be questioned, and after waiting the required 48 hours, you had her cremated, thus removing all traces of your crime. It was classic; a perfect crime if her friends hadn't decided to make a fuss and hire me to look into it."

"No, that's not true," she cried. "I didn't kill her. I gave her a piece of the cake when she asked for it, that's true, but I didn't give her anything else, and I haven't touched a penny from her estate; you can check the books."

"Don't worry, I will. In the meantime, I'll be reporting this to the local authorities. You'll have a lot of questions to answer when I do."

Tears were flowing down her cheeks now, and her shoulders were slumped.

"No, no, this is wrong. I didn't do anything."

"Teresa, how could you?" Winthrop asked.

"She didn't do anything," Dunn said levelly.

"So, stop picking on her."

Her voice was cold and level; and she glared first at Winthrop, then at me.

"You two are just like that bitch at school. Teresa did not kill Geraldine Wallace."

"How can you know that, Wilomena?" Winthrop asked.

She took a deep breath and turned to face him, looking up at him with hatred in her eyes.

"You bastard; you've been trying to undercut her from the start; always questioning her decisions. You'd like nothing better than to see her disgraced and fired wouldn't you? Well, it won't happen. She didn't do it."

"How do you know this?" I asked gently.

"Because, I did it," she said.

Chapter 33

The cops had driven into the parking lot after I passed, and as soon as Dunn uttered her confession, they came in and cuffed her.

She began giving a detailed confession while they were reading her Miranda Rights, and despite the lead detective warning her that she had the right to remain silent and urging her to do so, it poured out in torrents.

When she noticed the tension between Winthrop and Arden, her protective instincts had kicked in. She knew of the struggle between the two of them for control of the center, and was also aware of Arden's money problems. Fearing that this would lead to yet another failure and rejection, she determined to help.

Over the months she'd come to know Winthrop's habits well, and when she'd seen Wallace eating in the dining room, especially after the woman had asked for some of Arden's proffered chocolate cake, a plan formed in her mind.

As luck would have it, the combination of food and beer had, in fact, given the old woman a bad case of indigestion; bad enough for her to seek Dunn out for something to ease the discomfort.

She'd given her a placebo instead of antacid, which, as she knew it would, hadn't eased the pain, and while Winthrop had his back turned to wash his hands, had injected a large dose of phenelyzine, concealing the syringe in her scrubs. She hadn't known that the woman's body would be cremated; had hoped, in fact, that a subsequent examination would reveal the chemicals in her system, leading to Winthrop being charged with malpractice and getting the boot.

When that hadn't happened, she was at a loss until I showed up.

She'd been silently cheering me on when it looked like I was focusing on Winthrop's incompetence, hoping that it would stir up enough controversy and questions to achieve her original aim.

I learned later that during the ride to the Montgomery County Jail, she'd confessed to having done the same thing four previous times when she thought Winthrop was threatening

Arden's position, each time the bodies had been cremated, causing her plan to undermine him to fail.

In a conversation with the detective when I went to police headquarters to give my own statement, he said her matter-of-fact recitation of what she'd done had given him the chills. She had no ill feelings toward any of her victims, she'd told the cops, in fact, no feelings at all. They were old people who had little time left in any case, and their early demise was meant to serve a greater purpose. He said she told it as calmly as if she'd been describing putting down a terminally ill animal.

I can only wonder what she might have done had I failed in my investigation. And, when I thought about how close I'd come to doing just that, it gave me the chills.

William Powderly and his friends invited me to Shady Grove on Sunday, June 11; a sunny day, with a bright blue sky dotted with a few fluffy white clouds; to attend a memorial service for their friend.

After the service, attended by everyone at the center, including Morgan Winthrop and Teresa Arden, he and his two friends took me aside.

"I want to thank you, young fella," he said. "Everything that young lady assistant of yours said about you is true. You're one hell of a detective."

Helen Anthony wiped tears from her cheeks and craned up to plant a kiss on mine. "That's for sure," she said. "You're the only one who would listen to us, and you never gave up. We'll never forget what you did."

"You've really honored Geraldine's memory," George Madison said.

"Any time you feel like a game of cards," Powderly said. "We can always use a fourth."

I had a feeling the three of them would be playing cards together for a long time; and, I just might drop in from time to time to sit in on a hand or two.

Chapter 34

The British novelist Aldous Huxley said, 'Most human beings have an almost infinite capacity for taking things for granted.' He could have added that most human beings also have difficulty letting go of the assumptions they make.

I'd started this case by making some assumptions, all of which turned out to be mistaken.

The truth, like Poe's 'Purloined Letter,' was in plain sight all along, but, I'd missed it, and in doing so had almost let a cold-hearted serial killer go free.

I hadn't awakened Sandra to go with me to the memorial service, which had been held just after dawn, according to Powderly, Geraldine Wallace's favorite time of day. The smell of bacon frying greeted me when I opened the door.

Sandra was in the kitchen, dressed in cutoff jeans and a tank top, at the stove removing crisp looking strips of bacon from a skillet. Stacks of golden brown pancakes were on two plates at the little table near the stove where we usually had our breakfast; in this case, since it was approaching ten, our brunch. The smell of fresh-brewed coffee caressed my nose.

I walked up behind her and slipped my arms around her waist, pulling her back against me, reveling in the warmth of her against my body.

"Promise me," I said. "When I get old, you won't desert me, or pack me away in some sterile place for old people."

She twisted around and stuck a slice of bacon in my mouth, and then kissed away the smear of bacon grease.

"You'll never get old, love; or, at least, no older than you were when you were born. And, you know, you were born old."

I swallowed the bacon and kissed her back. "What's that supposed to mean?"

"You are a deep thinker. I think you've probably always been one. You see and feel things the rest of us miss. That means you have a mind that's ancient in scope. On the other hand, you're a person of action. That's rare in the same individual, and that makes you unique. People like you don't age like ordinary mortals."

"I don't know if I'm comfortable with that. That means the rest of the world will age around me, and I'll be left as an outcast."

She ground her pelvis against me. "Never, babe," she said. "You will always be mine. At the same time, you'll also always belong to the rest of the world. You're the one who comes to our rescue, even when sometimes we don't know we need rescuing. How did the memorial go?"

It had, in fact, been a nice ceremony; and for someone like me who has never liked funerals, that's saying something. I told her about the invitation for me to visit.

"And, even though you're still not comfortable around people with infirmities, you'll do it. I know you. Maybe I'll go along now and then as well."

"Yeah, I'll go. You know, I think I got over my issues with age. Watching people like Bill Powderly, made me realize that age is a state of mind. I never met Geraldine Wallace, but I got to know her nonetheless. She might have been living in a 90-year-old body, but mentally and spiritually, she was still a young woman; so are her friends. It's tempting to describe them as kids trapped in old bodies, but that's not the way they see themselves. I've been making the mistake of judging by external appearances.

They gave me a glimpse behind the curtain."

"And, unlike the rest of us, you have this amazing capacity to recognize the problem and find a solution. That's what both endears me to you and frightens me at the same time."

"Frightens you? How? Why?"

"Because, I'm afraid I won't be able to live up to it."

I pulled her close. Her head rested on my shoulder.

"That's one thing you don't have to worry about, sweetheart," I said into her hair. "You're everything I could ever hope for and more. Make you a deal; we'll grow old together."

I hope the world's ready for that.

DON'T MISS . . . .

THE WHITE DRAGONS

COMING SOON!

The black ZIL threw up a rooster tail of dust as it sped along the winding dirt track that passed for a road.

The sun was a semi-circle of dull orange, handing in a dead gray sky behind the jagged peaks of the mountains to the west, casting elongated purple shadows over the bleak and desolate landscape.

There were few trees; a few stunted saplings, gnarled and twisted by the wind, hunched over the parched earth like ancient gnomes, their roots penetrating deep into the earth in search of the rare underground pool of water. Here and there, small flocks of sheep that had spent the day grazing on the rough grass that was scattered about the dry ground were being driven back to the cabins made of blackened logs, to be lodged in pens attached to them, pens made of the same misshapen logs. The rest of the livestock, one or two skinny cows, maybe a pig or two, and some chickens, ducks, and rabbits, would already be in the back room of the little four-room hut which they shared with the farmer's family. The family, except for the farmer and perhaps his oldest sons, would already be huddled in the central room, around the clay oven for warmth, for even in early May, the night air was cold.

The three men in the ZIL, though, paid no attention to any of this. The driver kept his eyes on the road ahead, ready to brake should a flock of sheep suddenly appear. Seated in the back, two men sat, each on his own side, back against the door, speaking quietly.

"Are you sure this is a wise thing to do, Vasily?" the younger of the two, a clean-shaven man in his mid-twenties, wearing a gray suit and a white shirt that was open at the collar.

His companion was in his late forties. He had a high forehead, with his hairline somewhere near to crown of his skull, jet black hair combed straight back and down. Piercing brown eyes sat on either side of a thin nose that hung like a hawk's beak over thin lips set in a neatly trimmed moustache and pointed goatee. Vasily Shermov looked like Vladimir Ilyich

Lenin, and was proud of the resemblance, even taking to wearing dark suits like the Russian Communist leader. He laughed, harsh and guttural, spraying spittle across the seat.

"There is nothing to worry about, Pyotr," he said. "My cousin, Dmitri, will certainly approve of what I'm doing."

"And, if he does not approve?"

The question hung in the air like a threat. Shermov didn't need to answer; both he and his young assistant, Pyotr Ksolvi, knew the answer to that question; they would simply be made to disappear, to vanish from the face of the earth as if they'd never existed. Shermov's cousin, Dmitri Kovasc, was the First Secretary and head of the Central Committee of the Dagastan Soviet, and concurrently, head of the dreaded Dagastani Secret Service. He'd been merely the chief intelligence officer for ten years until he'd engineered the overthrow and murder of the former First Secretary and assumed that position as well.

Dmitri, Shermov knew, did not tolerate opposition or failure, and he had only one response to either; a response that was final and fatal.

Dagastan, a small landlocked country straddling the Arctic Circle in the near west of the USSR, surrounded by Russia, with the Cherskiy Range to the east and the Indigirka

River to the far west, it was little more than a dot on the Russian map, about the size of the American state of New Hampshire, with a population of slightly over one million. Its people were mainly nomadic herdsmen and hunters, scratching out a living from undernourished flocks of sheep or from trapping animals for fur in the remaining forests at the foot of the mountains.

The main ethnic group, the Kazbektuni, for whom the country's capital, Kazbektun, was named, was a result of intermarriage of Rus, the light-skinned invaders from Scandinavia, and Khan, the descendants of the Mongol invaders from the east. Although they accounted for sixty percent of the population, they were among the poorest of the poor, mostly subsistence farmers, herdsmen, or trappers. In the entire governing structure of Dagastan, a bloated bureaucracy of over one thousand officials, there were only two Kazbektuni, both low level functionaries. The country's ruling Central Committee had one Kazbektuni, an elderly man who spent most meetings with his head back, sound asleep. Among the menials; drivers, janitors, and other laborers, the Kazbektuni were vastly in the majority. The ZIL's driver was Kazbektuni. While he understood the Russian his two passengers were speaking, his preference was to speak his native Dagastani.

The Khan ethnic group made up ten percent

of Dagastan, and remained mostly on the vast desolate steppe, herding sheep and living in conical tents made of sheepskin, after the manner of their Mongol ancestors. Aggressive and militaristic, they held ten positions in the Central Committee's membership of one hundred. Short of leg, and barrel chested, they had the broad foreheads, slanted eyes, and flat noses of the Mongols. They were excellent horsemen, and it was said that one Khan soldier was worth fifty other Dagastani. Over time, the Khan had come to speak Russian, but with a thick accent.

The remaining thirty percent of the population was Rus, the descendants of Norse invaders who hadn't stopped in Russia, but had pushed on toward the west. They tended to light skins, brown or blond hair, high foreheads, and superior airs. Rus held all leadership positions that counted, including control of the intelligence, army, and police. The country's central bank was in the hands of a Rus, and most of its preferred customers were Rus.

Vasily Shermov and Pyotr Ksolvi were Rus, and had grown up speaking only Russian. Shermov knew a few words, but his young companion knew not one. Vasily was an official of the economic planning committee, and he'd come across information that would, he felt certain, change the future of Dagastan.

He hadn't taken news of his discovery to his

superior or to his cousin, wanting to verify it first, and then ensure that things were arranged in a way that ensured the future prosperity of all of Dagastan's people. If he could get everything lined up properly, he felt sure his cousin would forgive his breech of protocol.

The sudden deceleration of the ZIL, and a muttered curse in Dagastani from the front seat, startled both men.

"What is it, Leonid?" Shermov demanded.

"Flock of sheep in the road," the driver said in horribly-accented Russian.

"Well, drive around them, fool. We must make our schedule."

"Sorry, sir; is not good idea. The ground off the road can be tricky. We might get stuck. The flock will pass soon."

"Well, it better," Shermov said, and settled back, turning his attention to his companion.

He didn't see, therefore, the driver, Leonid, reach over and flick the light switch quickly, blinking the headlights. Nor did he see the four shadowy figures dressed entirely in black that emerged from behind the flock, menacing looking AK-47s held across their chests. They wore balaclava masks pulled down over their faces.

Two moved to the left and two to the right,

stopping at the passenger windows. Pyotr Ksolvi was the first to see them, and his eyes opened with fright. Noticing his young companion's expression, Vasily looked up, and his mouth dropped open. "What the bloody hell?" he said, and turned toward the front.

Before he could complete the turn, the four men, aiming downward to avoid hitting their companions, released a deadly stream of bullets shattered the windows of the ZIL and tore into the soft flesh of the two men, tossing them around the seat like limp puppets. Blood spattered the car interior.

It happened so quickly, neither man had had time for more than the beginning of a scream of terror before silent darkness descended. The two corpses lay entwined like two lovers, their facial features unrecognizable after being ripped and shredded by the force of the projectiles.

A pale of gray smoke hung over the car and the smell of cordite was thick. The driver reached for the door handle. One of the men on his side put his hand on the door, jamming it shut.

"I'm sorry, Leonid," he said, his voice muffled by the mask. "But, we must make this look like it was an act of terror, and there must be no way of it being linked to us." He spoke in Dagastani.

Leonid's mouth dropped open. "But, I was promised – -"

His words were cut off by the staccato drum beat of the man's AK-47, which tore through the driver's window, showering him with shards of grass milliseconds before his chest was torn apart by the projectiles. He was thrown back against the far door, his face frozen in an expression of disbelief.

The taller of the black-clad men took a dirty, oil-stained gray bricklike shape from his pocket and, walking around to the rear of the ZIL, stuffed it into the space between the exhaust pipe and the gas tank. He then inserted a short fuse, and using a battered lighter, lit.

"Let us get out of here," he said. "The fuse is good for two minutes."

The others ran toward the front of the car, shooting and yelling at the sheep to move them. Some of the animals ignored the noise and continued to graze on the rough grass. The four men ran flat out until they were about two hundred meters from the hulking shape of the ZIL. The sky had darkened considerably, but was suddenly lightened by the orange fireball of the ZIL being tossed into the air as the block of C-4 explosive detonated and the fumes from the gas tank ignited. The noise of the initial explosion was loud, but the explosion of the gas tank was deafening. The car was quickly engulfed in flames, spreading an orange glow in a circle expanding out several yards. Black smoke billowed upwards. Along with the smell of burning petrol, there was the sweet smell of roasting flesh.

The sheep that had not been killed by the concussion, or roasted in the ensuing fire, fled across the dusty ground, bleating in panic and kicking up a cloud of dust as they stampeded toward the safety of the hills. The four men stood in silence, gazing at their handiwork. After a few minutes, the tall man spun on his heels and started walking toward the hills. The others followed.

The incident wasn't known of or reported in Dagastan's capital city of Kazbektun for two days, and only after two Khan tribesmen had come upon the still smoldering wreckage. Outside Dagastan, it didn't even rate a small space in any international media.

But, in a short span of time, it would have international impact.

ABOUT THE AUTHOR

Charles Ray has been writing fiction since his teens, winning a national Sunday school magazine writing contest while still in junior high school. He worked as a newspaper and magazine journalist during the 1960s and 1970s, contributing articles, reviews, photographs, and artwork to a number of publications in the U.S. and abroad. His first full length work was a book on leadership, *Things I Learned from My Grandmother About Leadership and Life,* published in 2008. In 2009, he returned to his first love, fiction, with the first in a mystery series, *Color Me Dead.* He has since penned more than 20 fiction and non-fiction works.

A native of Texas who now calls Maryland home, he served 20 years in the U.S. Army, and upon retirement in 1982 joined the U.S. Foreign Service. Until his retirement from public service in 2012, he served throughout the world, but continued to write, frequently contributing to print and on-line publications along with writing fiction and non-fiction. He was a featured travel writer for Yahoo Voices on-line until the featured writer program was terminated, but is still a regular writer for various Yahoo sites, and is diplomatic correspondent for Asnycnow, a New York City based internet radio station. He is also an avid blogger whose work can be found at http://charlesaray.blogspot.com and http://charlieray45.wordpress.com.

While serving as U.S. Ambassador to

Zimbabwe, Ray contributed a number of op-eds to local media, which the U.S. Embassy published as a book for young people, *Where you come from matters less than where you're going*, which was distributed to schools and youth groups in English and two of the main tribal languages, Shona and Ndebele.

For more information on his published works, check his author page at http://www.amazon.com/Charles-Ray/e/B006WMLEZK or follow his tweets at http://www.twitter.com/charlieray45.